Also By Liliana Rhodes

His Every Whim
His Every Whim, Part 1
His One Desire, Part 2
His Simple Wish, Part 3
His True Fortune, Part 4
The Billionaire's Whim - (boxed set)

Canyon Cove
Playing Games
No Regrets
Second Chance
Hearts Collide
Perfect Together

Made Man Trilogy
Soldier
Capo
Boss

Gambino Family Novels
Dante (Made Man Trilogy boxed set)
Sonny

The Crane Curse Trilogy
Charming the Alpha
Resisting the Alpha
Needing the Alpha
The Crane Curse Trilogy Boxed Set

Wolf at Her Door
His Immortal Kiss

HEARTS COLLIDE

Liliana Rhodes

Published by
Jaded Speck Publishing
5042 Wilshire Blvd #30861
Los Angeles, CA 90036

Hearts Collide
A Canyon Cove Novel
Copyright © 2016 by Liliana Rhodes
Cover by CT Cover Designs

ISBN 978-1-939918-29-1

This book is a work of fiction. The names, characters, places, and incidents are products of the writer's imagination or have been used fictitiously and are not to be construed as real. Any resemblance to persons, living or dead, actual events, locales or organizations is entirely coincidental.

All rights reserved. No part of this book may be reproduced, scanned, or distributed in any manner whatsoever without written permission from the author except in the case of brief quotation embodied in critical articles and reviews.

Dedication

To S,
I love you lots and lots.

Prologue

Jackie

It was a perfect June day in Canyon Cove. The sun was beginning to set into the Pacific Ocean and one of my best friends just married the love of her life. Things couldn't be better.

I sat at a table in the corner of the large patio facing the beach, admiring the view. It was a small wedding and even though I was happy for Samantha and Drake, I couldn't deny the emptiness I felt. I looked at my new friend with his warm brown eyes and silky black hair and smiled.

"There's nothing like a romantic beach wedding. And of course to heighten the romance even more it has to happen at sunset, with the orange haze of the sun glittering perfectly off the calm ocean," I said as a bird squawked.

"Just ignore the seagulls flying overhead, cackling to each other about the cake they're ready to dive bomb. Or the sand flying into everyone's eyes and hair with the gentle breeze," I added, dryly.

"Why are you looking at me like that?" I asked, tilting my head to mirror my friend. "No, I'm not bitter. Trust me when I say that getting married is the last thing on my mind. Sure, I like to play the game and ooh and ahh over the diamond engagement rings and fancy place settings no one ever uses, but it's not something I even think about.

"Really, I am ecstatic for Samantha and Drake. I mean look at her, she is literally glowing. And with that red hair, she's giving the sun a run for its money. Everything turned out perfect for her -- she got her fairy tale, her prince, her perfect June beach wedding. I just wish she'd lay off trying to fix me up with the best man. I need a boyfriend like I need a hole in my head," I said.

"I don't need it. I don't want it," I said, waving my hand in front of me. "Dating is too complicated. And it'll just distract me from the things that are important to me like finishing my Masters in Social Work. I'm thirty, I have a lot going on in my life. I could care less if I ever get married."

I stopped to admire my companion's quizzical look.

"You're looking at me like I'm crazy, but it's true," I said. "I don't want to get married. I don't even want a boyfriend. Well, not unless he's battery-powered."

I laughed as I scratched my new friend's wide head. His tongue rolled out of his mouth as he panted happily.

"You have it easy, my friend," I said as the dog tilted his head. "No, no, you keep giving me that look, but trust me when I say that life is much easier for you than it is for me."

He nudged the plate in my lap and then looked at me with his big brown eyes. I broke off a small piece of cheese and held it out to him. With his tail wagging, he took the cheese and swallowed it whole.

"I had a Lab like you about five years ago," I said. "He loved cheese. Actually loved everything and everyone, he wasn't very picky."

I handed him another small piece of cheese as he drooled a little on my blue dress.

"There you are, Shade." A man's voice came from behind me. It was smooth and deep and even without seeing who it was, it made my heart skip.

I turned around and recognized Mr. Best Man himself, Brent Winslow. Brother of the groom and my dream guy, at least according to Samantha.

"I trained him to find the most beautiful women wherever we go," Brent said as he flashed a perfect smile at me.

I rolled my eyes.

"Does that ever work?" I asked.

"He found you, didn't he?"

"No, I meant the line," I said.

He laughed, and small crinkles appeared at the corners of his smoky gray eyes and around his mouth. Samantha was right, he was a really good-looking man. Better than good-looking, he was hot. But it was obvious he knew that.

Brent was a human Ken doll with his perfect blond hair parted on the side, square jaw, chiseled cheekbones, and broad shoulders. The fact that he was wearing a dusty blue guayabera shirt and pale linen pants didn't help. I could easily imagine him living in a hot pink box at the toy store. Malibu Brent.

I didn't know what Samantha was thinking by saying he was perfect for me. I definitely was not a Barbie.

Pushing some loose strands of my brown hair back behind my ear, I looked back at my conversation partner, who was eyeing the rest of the cheese on my plate.

"Was he the only date you could get for the wedding?" I asked as I scratched Shade under his chin.

"I don't need a date," Brent said. "I'm the best man, remember? As maid of honor, you're practically required to sleep with me."

"I wasn't talking to you," I said, turning towards Brent. "I was talking to Shade." I turned my attention back to Shade. "You know, you really could do a lot better."

"At least I have a date," Brent said, grinning.

"Figures you would bring a dog as a date. You probably read something about it in GQ or something."

"You seem to keep forgetting that I'm the best man," he said. "I don't need a date. But maybe I should have brought you instead of Shade."

"Are you saying I'm a dog? No offense, Shade," I said.

"If I didn't think you were attractive, like I said before, I'm the best man. I can take my pick from the single women. Look at all the ladies lining up for me."

He opened his arms wide as he laughed, then sat down next to me.

This guy is too much, I thought.

"You realize there's less than fifty people here, right?" I said. "And you're related to some of them. That lessens your chances."

He shrugged.

"What do I need anyone else for when I have you, Miss Maid of Honor?" he said.

I slumped back in my chair and groaned.

"You cannot be serious," I said.

"Hmm I can see my charm isn't working on you." He looked at his dog and leaned closer to him. "Shade, I thought you would've softened her up for me." He looked at me out of the corner of his eye and grinned.

His charm *was* working on me. With his goofy lines and obvious confidence, how could I not like him? Plus, he had a dog, which said a lot about him.

Samantha might be right this time. Maybe he is perfect for me, I thought.

"So why are you hiding out here away from the rest of the party?" Brent asked.

"I don't know. I saw this spot and it seemed right."

"How do you know Sam?" he asked. "You know she and I grew up together. She's practically my sister."

"That's just gross. Your brother married his sister?" I widened my eyes in mock horror.

Everyone knew of the Winslow family. They were the oldest and wealthiest family in Canyon Cove. Samantha had told me a long time ago how, since her mother was the Winslow nanny, she grew up with them. Drake was the oldest by several years, so while Sam grew up with Brent and his sister Amber, she secretly daydreamed about Drake, who didn't know she existed.

"Well, you know what they say," he said. "Anything goes in Canyon Cove."

"Really? And who are they? Do I know these people?"

Brent laughed.

"I like you. You're funny," he said.

"Mmm...funny? That's exactly the last thing every girl wants to hear from an attractive man."

"Really? The last thing? I thought maybe 'is your friend single?' or what about 'wow that's the same dress my great aunt Sylvia wore for her eightieth birthday party.'" He laughed. "I could play this game for hours. How about 'you're gorgeous, do you have a twin brother?'"

"Okay, you win," I said. "Any of those would be worse than being called funny."

"Good. I like winning," he said. "You are funny though. And gorgeous, but no, I'm not interested in any brother you might have or your friend. And that dress does not look like anything my aunt Sylvia would wear. At least I hope not."

"Why?"

"Because with my luck, I'd be dreaming about you and then Aunt Sylvia would take your place and--" He shivered and shook his head. "No, just no."

"Seriously though, you look stunning," he added. "I'm used to seeing you with the ponytail and black and white catering uniform. I've never even seen your shoulders until tonight."

"I'm wearing a clingy dress and you're only noticing my shoulders?" I laughed.

"It's not all I'm noticing," he said. "But I'd be lying if I said I wasn't thinking about tearing those flimsy straps off."

His eyes met mine and everything stopped. There wasn't a setting sun on a beautiful beach or a party going on, it was just the two of us.

Shade whined as he wagged his tail.

"Okay, okay," Brent said to Shade as he stood, his eyes still locked on mine. "Shade would like to go for a walk. Do you want to join us?"

"Sure," I said as he held out his hand to me. "I just need a jacket. It's getting chilly."

The back wall of Drake and Samantha's house was open, letting people move in and out easily. Samantha was sitting down with her feet up. She had been suffering with swollen ankles in her last trimester of pregnancy. As I entered the house with Brent and Shade behind me, she nudged Drake, who was sitting beside her, and gave me a knowing smile.

I'll never hear the end of this.

Knowing Sam wouldn't mind my borrowing something of hers, I opened the large coat closet. Two rows of coats lined the walls like a mini department store. I shook my head in awe.

"My brother has always been obsessed with clothing," Brent said.

He was standing close behind me. With my hair up, his breath tickled the back of my neck, giving me goose bumps.

"Jackie," Samantha called out. "Where'd she go?"

Oh no!

I spun around and landed in Brent's arms. There were definitely worse places to be, but that made it even worse. I didn't want Samantha to catch us together.

"If she catches us together..." I said.

"She'll never let up," Brent said, completing my sentence.

The soft shuffle of slippers moved closer. Brent pushed me into the closet with him and pulled the door closed behind us.

"Where did they go?" Samantha said, sounding closer.

The absurdity of it hit me and I started to laugh. I covered my mouth with my hands as I tried to control myself, but it just made it worse.

As my eyes adjusted to the darkness, I noticed Brent's eyes widened and darted towards the door as if he was telling me to shut up. It made me laugh even more.

"Jackie?" Samantha called out, sounding confused.

I imagined her looking around and it made it even funnier. I couldn't help myself. Looking up at Brent, I could see him trying to hold back his own laughter. He held his finger up to his lips.

"Shhh," he whispered.

"I can't," I said, still fighting back my laughter.

He pulled me close to him, a smile on his face as he laughed quietly. Our eyes met like they did outside and the laughter stopped. His gray eyes were intense as my breath caught in my throat.

"Maybe we should take advantage of this closet," he said.

He cupped my face with his hands as his lips closed down on mine. He sucked my bottom lip before his tongue explored my mouth.

We moved against the door and he pressed his body against mine. He felt strong and muscular as my hand moved over his chest to his shoulders.

Slowly, his hands moved down my neck and over my breasts. His fingers moved over my hard nipples, making the thin fabric of the dress nonexistent. A small voice in my head said things were moving too fast, but I didn't care. It had been too long since I had been with a man, much too long since the last time I felt wanted.

His hand continued their trek down my body, reaching my hips, then following the curve of my butt. He lifted my dress as his lips brushed against my neck and shoulders. His hands skimmed my thighs before finding my panties and slipping a hand inside. As his lips met mine again, his fingers rubbed my wetness.

"Not here," I gasped.

"Why not?" he said huskily.

"She's right out there. And even if she goes away, someone might find us."

"Then that's even more of a reason to stay here," he said. "That makes it more fun."

His lips moved to a half smile and I knew he was up to something. "I want you to come." His finger slid into me and my body trembled, responding to his touch. "Come for me, here and now, and afterwards we can go wherever you want."

The whoosh of Samantha's slippers went past, then several voices approached, growing louder as they moved closer.

"What if they want their coats?" I murmured.

"Shhh." His finger moved deeper into me and I moaned. "You need to be quiet or they'll hear you. Do you want to come?"

I nodded as the voices stopped right outside the door. He curled his finger inside me and my body pulsed in response. I didn't want him to stop, but I couldn't stop listening to the voices in the hall.

"I think it's locked," a man's voice said as the door knob twisted, before Brent held it steady. "Maybe Drake has the key."

The voices grew faint. Brent withdrew his finger and rubbed it over my swollen clit. My breath came quickly. I wrapped my arms around his broad shoulders to hold myself up as my legs grew weak.

"Are you close?" he whispered.

His other hand cupped one of my breasts and squeezed my nipple between his fingers, pushing me closer to the edge. Panting, I nodded.

"I need to taste you," he said.

He knelt before me and rested my leg on his shoulder. He pushed my panties aside as his tongue teased me, sending a shockwave through my body. He moved his tongue faster over my clit until the wave of my orgasm crashed against me. I clutched at him as my body pulsed intensely.

Oh fuck, he is the best man.

As he stood, he smoothed my dress down, then grinned.

"Let's go," he said. "I'm not done with you."

"We can't leave, what about Sam?"

"Right now she's the last thing on my mind," he said. "But if it means that much to you, then I'll leave and wait in my car for you."

I shook my head. "This is crazy."

He cupped my face and kissed me again. Slowly his tongue entered my mouth and I leaned against him.

"Let's go," he said reaching for the closet door.

"No, not like this," I said thinking about his jokes earlier about being the best man. "Not today."

"Then how about tonight?" he asked.

I laughed. "No, if there's anything really between us it can wait for another day."

"Then give me your number," he said as he pulled out his cell phone. "So we can make plans for tomorrow."

"I'm not going to sleep with you," I said.

"Is that a challenge?"

"I'm being serious. After what you said before, there's no way. Not this fast."

"That doesn't change anything," he said. "I still want to see you tomorrow. And probably the day after that too."

"Why?"

"I don't know, but I want to find out. There's just something about you, Jackie Stone."

"How do you know my last name? Did Sam tell you?"

"There's a lot I know about you," he said with a grin. "I'll just leave it at that."

I took his cell phone and entered my phone number. I didn't say it, but there was something about him too. Even though we didn't know each other well, it felt like I had known Brent my entire life.

"Sometimes you need to let it ring a lot before the answering machine kicks on," I said as I handed him his cell phone back.

"Answering machine? What year do you live in?" he teased.

"Very funny," I said. "It's a long story, but I'm waiting for a replacement phone. Until then, I only have my landline."

"Alright, this better be a real number," he said as he put his cell phone away.

"Are you ever serious?" I asked.

"Rarely. Life is too short to be serious."

After we left the closet, Brent decided to go home. He walked over to me with a naughty smirk and I thought he was going to kiss me again, but then he held out his hand for me to shake.

"We're shaking hands?" I asked.

"Sam's watching and we're not close enough to the closet," he said before speaking loudly. "It was wonderful meeting you. What did you say your name was again?"

"Jackass."

"You're much too pretty for the name Jackass," he whispered.

"No, you're a jackass," I said, laughing.

"Stop laughing, you don't know what it does to me. I'll have to toss you over my shoulder and carry you back to the closet."

"Don't you think Sam will get suspicious that you're still shaking my hand all this time?"

He turned and looked at Sam, who grinned and waved.

"I suspect she's onto us," he said. "I'll give you a call about tomorrow."

I won't hold my breath, I thought.

He seemed too good to be true. He was incredibly hot, had a great sense of humor, was a great kisser, and had a dog. *Why would he call me? If he's as perfect as Sam says, why wasn't he already taken?*

I knelt to pet Shade and he gave me his paw.

"Guess he wants to shake your hand too," Brent said.

I spent the rest of the evening thinking that I should have left the party with him. I should have thrown caution to the wind and done something even more wild and crazy for once. What did I care what Samantha would say? There was no way she would keep pushing him on me if things didn't work out.

**

A week later, I was visiting Sam when the inevitable came up.

"Alright, Jackie," she said as she sat on the lounger on the patio. "I've been waiting for you to spill the beans, but you haven't said anything yet and it's driving me crazy."

I knew what she was talking about, but I figured however long I could put it off, the better.

"Spill the beans? You mean about my new phone? It's a lot nicer than the last one, but the bean thing didn't work on drying the old one out."

"That's not beans, it's rice. You put your wet phone in rice. I doubt that works either though," she said. "Wait a minute, you know I have major pregnancy brain. Don't try to confuse me. Have you gone out with Brent yet? I saw you two at the wedding, I knew you'd hit it off."

Sighing, I leaned back in my chair and sipped from my glass of fresh lemonade. The day was perfect with blue skies and the ocean gently lapping the shore. Having to talk about him was definitely making the day take a wrong turn.

"We're not going out. Ever," I said.

"Ever? I don't understand. I saw the spark. I know something happened in that closet. What do you mean you're never going out with him?"

"He's an asshole," I said.

"No, he's not, he's great. What happened? This has to be a misunderstanding."

"Remember, you know a different Brent than I do. You never had to date him."

"I know him well enough to know he's not an asshole," she said. "Just tell me what happened. I'm sure there's a simple explanation."

"There is. He's a total jerk who didn't call. He said he was going to. He said he wanted to see me the next day, but then he didn't even bother calling."

"Okay, okay," she said. "Calm down."

"You know how this brings it all back. I can't help that. I wish it didn't, especially since it's been so long, but if a guy can't even call, then how can I trust him?"

"I'm really surprised he didn't call," Samantha said. "That's not like him at all. You gave him your cell?"

"No, I didn't have my new phone yet so I gave him my home number."

"Maybe your answering machine is on the fritz," she said. "You've had that thing for years."

"I get other messages. Besides, Dennis is there all the time. He answers the phone when I'm not home."

"Dennis? Are you freaking kidding me? I can't believe you."

"It's not what you think," I said. "I'm just helping him out. His landlord decided to sell the building, so he needed a place to stay until he finds a new place."

"Whatever, Jackie. You know he's got more excuses and stories than anyone."

I sighed. "He had nowhere else to go. I wasn't going to let him sleep on the street."

"Whatever," Sam said in a huff. "I just don't get you sometimes. After all the things he did."

"At least Dennis calls when he says he's going to."

"Did you ever think that maybe Dennis answered the phone and didn't tell you Brent called?"

"What? No, Dennis wouldn't do that. Why would he do that?" I asked.

Every day that week, I had asked Dennis if anyone called, and no one did. I didn't want to admit that to Samantha though. I didn't want anyone to know how hurt and disappointed I was that Brent didn't call. It was easier to put up the tough front than deal with how I felt. It's how I always handled things.

"Because that's exactly the douchey kind of thing Dennis would do. You know I don't trust him, and I never liked him. I always told you he was just a rebound after Marc. Why you kept going back to him for four years was beyond me. You're thirty, you should know better."

"We're not back together. Trust me on that," I said, thinking that talking about Brent was the lesser of two evils. "It doesn't change the fact that your brother-in-law is a jerk. I can't stand him. He's no different than Marc. I hope I never see him again."

Chapter One

Brent

It had been four months since Sam and my brother Drake's wedding. Every time I had seen Sam since then, she brought up Jackie and tried to get us together. I had managed to come up with an excuse for not attending Sam's matchmaking dinners, but this time I was out of luck.

As I pulled up to their house, I noticed Jackie's old car parked at the curb. The large vehicle stood out from the newer cars on the street and in the driveways. The paint was faded, making the once-black car look an unappealing dull grey color. I liked her car. It had character, just like Jackie.

I walked into the house without ringing the doorbell. Drake, Sam, and Jackie were already sitting at the dinner table eating. I didn't mean to show up late, but I had no choice.

Jackie looked up as I entered the room, turned away, and quickly looked back at me again.

"You brought someone?" she said, her face a mix of surprise and anger.

"Didn't you?" I asked.

Her face contorted, but she didn't say anything. She looked at my date, standing beside me with her arm curled around mine. Drake pushed his hand through his thick blond hair before shaking his head as he held back a laugh. Sam's face glowed with hot anger.

"I know it's customary to bring wine to a dinner party," I said as I held up a bottle of red wine. "But I also brought Brandi."

"Hello," Brandi said.

She wiggled her perfectly manicured fingers into the air as she tilted her head cutely to the side, making her long honey-colored tresses cascade over her shoulder. Brandi knew my brother had contacts in the entertainment industry. I knew she would work this opportunity as best as she could.

"Please sit, Brandi," Sam said politely. "Why don't you make yourself comfortable while I speak to Brent in the kitchen."

She rose to her feet, her mouth in a hard line. She forced a smile at Brandi and then shot me a death glare as she walked to the kitchen door.

"Sam, why don't you sit," I said. "I'll grab an extra place setting for myself. No need for you to go out of your way."

Sam's eyes widened in a way that reminded me of her mother, my nanny, growing up. I was in trouble.

"In. The. Kitchen. Now," she growled.

"I think I should go," Jackie said, pushing her chair back.

"Don't you dare move." Sam pointed at Jackie, who jerked her chair back into place.

I followed Sam to the farthest part of the kitchen where she spun around, her eyes wide.

"You suck," she said as she punched me in the arm.

"Really?" I said, rubbing my bicep. "Really, Sam? I can't believe you hit me."

"It felt good," she said with a shrug. "I should hit you again for Jackie."

"You haven't hit me since we were eight."

"You haven't done anything as stupid as this since then," she said. "How could you bring a date?"

"I'm sorry, I know it was stupid of me to do that, but you knew I didn't want to come."

"Why not? I saw you two at my wedding. Even before then, when you saw her at the Fitzsimmons's party I catered, you couldn't take your eyes off her. You asked me for her number then."

"And you said she was taken. You told me about that asshole Dennis she was dating," I said.

"She's not with him anymore," she said. "They broke up last year."

"Well, she's with someone else now."

Sam squinted at me. It was her *'you're completely insane'* look.

"What are you talking about? She's not with anyone," she said.

I shook my head. "Then she's keeping something from you."

Samantha's brow wrinkled. "What makes you think that?"

"I don't want to talk about it," I said. "But trust me on this."

I headed back towards the dining room where Jackie pushed food around on her plate while Brandi talked about the movies she had been an extra in.

"Let's get going," I said.

Brandi stopped talking mid-sentence. Her shoulders slumped as her face fell and her bottom lip slipped into a pout.

Annoying, I thought.

I didn't care about Brandi. I barely knew her. She was nothing like the women I liked to date, but I was hoping she would make Jackie feel a little of the jealousy I felt whenever I thought of her with someone else.

Jackie shot up to her feet.

"You don't have to go," she said. "I'll go."

She sped past me towards the coat closet. My instincts said to follow her, and I did.

"Just stay," I said. "I shouldn't have come anyway."

She reached into the closet and pulled out a black oversized sweater. I took the sweater from her and held it up to help her put it on, but she swiped it out of my hands.

"No, you shouldn't have come," she said. Her eyes darted over to Brandi and then back to me. "I'm glad nothing happened between us."

Her words slapped me and reminded me not only that she was taken, but also what I heard about her.

"I'm glad too," I said. "But then why are you here?"

"Just go away and leave me alone," she said.

"Fine, if that's what you want."

"You're such an asshole," she said.

"And you're a..." A hundred different words flashed through my head, but I couldn't bring myself to say any of them. No matter how much she angered me, I'd never call her something bad. "You're a witch."

She blinked at me while her brow knitted.

"I hate you," she said through clenched teeth.

While her words slapped me before, this time they stabbed at my heart.

She roughly shoved her arms into her sweater and turned towards the door. Sam appeared and they hugged after Jackie whispered something to her I couldn't hear.

As Jackie left, Sam gave me an evil look.

"What is wrong with you?" she said.

I shook my head and let out a long breath.

How could she hate me?

"I'm sorry, Sam," I said. "I really am."

Brandi slid beside me with a sparkly white smile.

"Okay, I'm ready," she said as she held up Drake's business card.

Sam rolled her eyes.

"I'm not done talking to you, Brent," she said.

"I know, okay? I'll call you tomorrow," I said.

Brandi talked non-stop as I drove along the dark, curving canyon road. Drake told her he knew someone filming a cable show that was looking for help and she was excited about the opportunity.

I didn't really pay attention to what she was saying. Drake made it a habit of helping everyone he met. That was the benefit he had of knowing so many people. Brandi could care less about me other than I was Drake Winslow's brother. It was okay, I could care less about her too.

But Jackie was a different story.

I hated thinking that I might have said or done something that hurt her tonight. I didn't know what I was doing anymore. Ever since Jackie and I had our fling at the wedding, all I thought about was her.

Sam was right to look at me like I was crazy. I was, and it was all Jackie's fault. She did something to me that made the most ridiculous ideas make sense to me. I sighed as I glanced at the ridiculous idea sitting next to me babbling.

"Where can I drop you off?" I asked, interrupting her.

"Drop me off? We're not going back to your place?" Brandi asked.

"No, this was just dinner, nothing else," I said.

Brandi gave me an address that was on the other side of town before she continued on about her career and how hard she's worked on it.

I turned on the car stereo, which picked up where it left off on my playlist. Sting was singing about his heart breaking with every step. I raised the volume to drown out the din of Brandi's voice.

Another ridiculous idea popped into my head. It was just crazy enough that it might work. I refused to let Jackie keep hating me, but could I make her like me and maybe love me someday? I'd do everything I could to find out.

Chapter Two

Jackie

The television blared from the living room. I closed my eyes and took a deep breath before leaving my bedroom, knowing that if I started yelling at Dennis now, I would never make it to lunch at Mirabella's on time.

Dennis O'Hara was my ex-boyfriend and sometime friend. We had been on and off for four years, with the last year or so off, and I had no plans on getting back together with him again.

He was an average-looking guy with short, spiky, mousey brown hair and glasses. Lately he had been sporting a soul patch, a tuft of hair in the middle of his chin, which I thought looked ridiculous but he thought looked cool.

It was football season, and Dennis never missed a game on TV. He tuned everything out while the game was on. He had already been staying with me a week, and I was ready for him to leave. In the past few months it seemed like he was staying with me more and more regularly, with one excuse after another. I hated it.

"Can't you just--" *Breathe Jackie, breathe.* "Could you please lower the volume? Mrs. Reilly has complained several times about the noise to the landlord."

Dennis turned to look up at me from his spot on the couch. He grabbed the remote and lowered the volume a little, then tossed the remote onto the cocktail table, making my hand-blown glass fish wobble. He roughly put his feet up on the table next to the fish.

If he knocks that over, I will kill him.

I fought the urge to move the fish, trying to give Dennis the benefit of the doubt for once, but I couldn't do it. I picked up the fish and gently placed it on my bookcase. I'd had that fish for ten years and Grandma had it for decades before that. It was my most prized possession. I couldn't risk his damn feet being anywhere near it. As I turned around, Dennis glared at me.

"You really think I'm a fuck-up, don't you?" he asked as he turned back to the TV.

"I think I love that fish and don't want it to break," I said, glad I didn't tell him off.

"It's a stupid, ugly glass fish," he said.

"It belonged to my grandmother. She gave it to me on my eighteenth birthday."

"Shitty gift," he muttered.

Bite your tongue, Jackie. Don't say another word or you'll be late.

I grabbed my cellphone and my bag and opened the door.

"Where are you going?" Dennis asked.

"Out," I said.

"But it's almost lunch."

"So? You're a big boy. I'm sure you can find something to eat."

"You never left me alone when we were dating," he said.

"We are not dating," I said angrily, turning towards him. "We haven't dated for a year now, and I will never date you again."

Dennis shrugged, his eyes still on the football game.

"Bring me back something?" he asked.

I sighed as I clenched my jaw. Saying yes would get me out of here quicker than arguing with him even more.

"What do you want?" I asked.

"A turkey sandwich. You know, like from that place you like going to that makes it with all the Thanksgiving fixings."

"Fine."

As I closed the door behind me, I heard him yell.

"And a Coke. You never have anything good here."

"If you want something good, then buy it yourself," I muttered angrily.

I got into my car and turned the key in the ignition. The car coughed, choked, and went silent. I tried it again, holding the key in the on position, letting the engine whine as I waited for it to turn on, but nothing happened.

Shit! Now what?

Staring blankly at the dashboard, I went through all the problems the old car could have.

Battery? No, it was making noise. Transmission? No, I had that replaced over the summer.

Letting out a long sigh, I got out of the car and looked at it, hoping it would magically start. There was no way I was getting to Mirabella's now.

A baby blue sports car zipped past, then screeched as it stopped at the corner. The engine roared as the driver hit the gas.

Asshole, I thought. *Probably another ridiculous billionaire. Like this town doesn't have enough of them.*

As I got back into my car, a car horn sounded. I ignored it and turned the key in the ignition again. The car still didn't start. The horn honked longer, so I rolled down my window and gave the guy the finger. It was the blue sports car. It honked again.

I opened the car door and stepped out, yelling at the expensive car.

"You can't have this spot. I'm not leaving. I can't leave, you fucking asshole!"

The car door opened, and Brent Winslow got out of the car wearing a pair of slacks with a white button-down shirt and a huge shit-eating grin.

Of all the people, why did it have to be him?

I jumped back into my car as he approached.

"You piece of shit," I yelled. "Now would be a good time to start. Now!"

"I wasn't trying to get your spot," Brent said as he leaned against my car door. "I already got your spot about four months ago, remember?"

He cocked his brow at me and I swore his eyes twinkled. Sometimes it was too easy to hate this man. Today just wasn't my day.

"Ugh, really?" I shook my head. "I'm reminded of it every time I see you."

"See, you can't stop thinking about it either," he said with a wink.

"Please, just stop. I don't need this right now. Can't you see I'm in the middle of something?"

"What's wrong with your car?" he asked.

"How do I know? It won't start. It's going to cost me a lot of money. That's how it always is with this car."

"Did you put gas in it?"

"Did I put gas in it." I rolled my eyes "Do I look stupid?"

My mind raced, trying to think about when I last put gas in the car. There's no way it was empty.

I glanced at the old car's dashboard and saw the red dial pointed to 'E'. *Dennis!* I let out a long sigh and hung my head down as I rubbed my forehead. Dennis had borrowed my car the other day. I should know better than to expect him to take care of it.

Stupid! Stupid!

"Okay then, how about you just let your car rest and I'll give you a ride?"

I turned and pointed at his car.

"In that?" I asked, scrunching my face.

"It's a really nice car," he said, opening my car door.

"I should've known you'd drive something that flashy, but baby blue? Really?"

"That's a special paint job. You won't find another Maserati GranTurismo in this color."

"There's a reason for that," I said. "Why would you get a car in this color?"

"I didn't, although I do have one, just not in this color. This was given to me as a gift, but I'm donating it to charity. I just figured I'd take it for a drive first."

"Which charity? The society of billionaire douchebags?"

"No, we don't accept gifts. We just have our monthly meetings where we talk about how we rescue damsels in distress. Looks like I'll have a good story to tell next time."

"I wasn't in distress," I said, folding my arms over my chest.

"Whatever you say," he said. "Hey, you want to drive it?"

"Really?" I asked, giving him the side eye. *What was he up to?*

"Sure, why not?" He handed me the keys, opened the driver's side door, and bowed. "My lady."

"I am not your lady, but thank you."

I lowered myself into the soft leather seats that hugged my body. I breathed deeply, taking in the new car smell. It was better than I imagined.

"Wow, I take it back, this is nice," I said.

"I told you it's a nice car. I think it'll bring in a pretty penny for the Humane Society."

"The Humane Society? You mean, like animal shelters and stuff like that?"

This guy can't be for real.

"Is there another one?" he said.

I steered the car back onto the street, enjoying the drive, when I realized I left my keys in my car's ignition. I shook my head and rolled my eyes while I silently yelled at myself.

"What's the matter?" Brent asked.

"I have to go back," I said, disappointed. "I swear I'm never getting to this lunch."

"Why?"

"I left my keys in the car." I looked in the rearview mirror as I tried to edge over into the next lane. "If I turn up here, I can probably loop back around."

"No, don't worry about it. You're going to Mirabella's, right?"

"Yes...how did you know?"

"That's not important," he said. "Just drive to the restaurant and I'll go back and get your keys for you."

"Listen, that's really nice, but you don't have to do that. Plus I thought you were busy."

"There's no deadline for charity," he said. "I'll get your keys and leave them with Amy. I'm sure you don't want to see me again."

I wanted to tell him that wasn't true but remembered how much I was supposed to hate him. I reminded myself how he said he would call and then didn't. Then I remembered that dinner where he brought a date, Brandi.

"I thought that was mutual," I said.

"It is. I don't want to see you either, but you know, I have to report a good deed to my Billionaire Douchebag Club."

"Oh, you're sooo funny," I said dryly.

I pulled into the parking lot behind Mirabella's, not wanting anyone to see me with him. That was all I needed. It was bad enough Samantha was always on my case for not thinking he was Prince Charming.

"Thanks for the ride," I said.

"And getting your keys."

"Well, you haven't done that yet."

"Oh, but I will, and then you'll really owe me," he grinned mischievously.

I couldn't help but smile back, but then I noticed the look in his eye. I recognized that look from the coat closet at Samantha's wedding. I couldn't forget that look. I didn't want to forget it.

Brent's hand reached behind my neck and pulled me closer to him. His lips closed over mine and I melted against him before realizing what I was doing. I pushed away from him and smacked his chest.

Damn, I forgot how muscular he is.

My mind spun with all the things I wanted to say to him--

Leave me alone!

Go away!

Get a life!

I'll be back in an hour.

There's a private bathroom in the restaurant.

Ever have sex in a car? Want to try now?

Instead I opened the car door and headed quickly towards the restaurant without looking back.

Chapter Three

Jackie

Mirabella's was unusually empty for a Saturday afternoon. I sat at the table surrounded by my friends, but I couldn't focus on what they were saying or anything at all. I stared at the rust-colored ceiling, then the art on the walls, then back at my plate.

I poked at my Cobb salad, grateful that Samantha was feeling especially chatty. As long as she kept talking, maybe no one would realize I was in my own world.

I hated that Brent had this effect on me. I hated that four months ago I had the best almost-sex I ever had and it was with a selfish, egotistical, gorgeous man who liked screwing women for the hell of it. And I hated that when I closed my eyes I could still feel his lips on my skin.

That kiss today, however brief, just made everything worse. It took me a while to stop obsessing about Brent and there I was doing it again.

"Hey, Jackie," Amy whispered as she tapped my shoulder.

Blinking, I brought myself back from my dream world and turned to look at her. Amy usually worked the cash register whenever we had our lunches there.

"Oh hey, Amy. I wasn't sure if you were working today. I didn't see you when I came in," I said.

"You walked right past me. You were in your own little world," she said with a soft laugh. "You'll have to tell me who is he another time, but he is very yummy. Like a young Robert Redford. Hot!" She fanned her face with her hand. "He just dropped off your keys."

She handed my keys to me and slipped away. I dropped them into my bag as I planned to go back to my home planet, but when I looked up

Samantha had an expectant gaze. I looked around the table and everyone was looking at me.

"What?" I asked.

"I swore I saw Brent come in and then Amy comes over and hands you keys," Samantha said. "I think I can speak for the table when I say we want details. Did you leave your keys at his place or is he leaving his keys with you?"

"Give me a break," I said. "You know I can't stand him, but yes that was him. They're my keys. I left them in my car."

"So why did he have them?"

I looked around the table hoping to find any excuse to talk about something else, but I came up blank.

"He was driving past and saw me fighting with my car," I said.

I shrugged hoping no one would point out what I was just realizing. It sounded ridiculous. *What was a wealthy man like Brent doing in my neighborhood?*

"Mmm hmm," Tara said.

The combination of her Southern accent and her raised eyebrow said more than words could have said. As I looked around the table, I could tell they were all thinking the same thing, that I was full of it.

"Really, I swear," I said. "My car wouldn't start and then Brent showed up and gave me a ride."

"Oh I'm sure he gave you a ride alright. Like the ride he gave you at my wedding," Samantha said with a laugh.

"Will you stop that? We didn't have sex. It amazes me sometimes how alike you two are with your jokes," I said, annoyed. "And really, you know it's not easy having to live up to my mistakes over and over. I don't bring up all the guys on your list. Can we just forget about it?"

"Umm, no," Samantha said as she tilted her head and grinned. "I'm willing to accept that he just so happened to be driving down the road you live on while your car wouldn't start. But when will you accept that fate is trying to get the two of you together?"

"What are you talking about fate? You think fate keeps making me run into him? If that's fate at work then she's even more of an idiot than I thought."

"Maybe fate was just giving you a taste of what's to come since you're going to see him again tomorrow," she said.

I stared at Samantha with my best *you've completely lost your mind* look.

"Why am I seeing him tomorrow?" I asked.

"Because you're coming over for dinner, remember? Brent is coming too."

"Wasn't last time bad enough? Why are you making me go through this again?"

"I'm telling you, Jackie, you guys would be great together," Samantha said. "You just need to spend more time with him. You have a lot in common and I know you don't like older men and Brent is only two years older than you."

I buried my head in my hands wishing she would stop talking about him. How long was she going to go on about him?

As we said our good-byes, I pulled Samantha aside as we left the restaurant.

"Can you give me a ride to the gas station and then home? I need to get my car running again," I said.

"What are you talking about? Isn't that your car right there?" she asked.

I looked towards where she was pointing and shook my head.

"That looks like my car, but I don't understand it. Dennis used my car the other day and didn't refill it for me. Maybe he realized that while I was gone and put some gas in it. He has my spare set of keys."

"Dennis?" Samantha said. "Why did you let him use your car? Don't even tell me you're back together with him. I don't know why you even bother with that asshole still. You've been on and off for four years now. Come on, Jackie, you know you deserve better."

"We're still off and there will never be an on again with him. I'm just trying to help him out," I said, opening the car door. "He's really not that bad. I mean look, the tank is full."

Samantha didn't say anything, but she didn't have to. Her face said it all. She didn't believe Dennis would do something nice. And if he did, then he would want something in return. That was how Dennis operated. I knew that, but I couldn't help but defend him.

***

Even though Dennis hadn't moved from where I left him, I still wanted to give him the benefit of the doubt. Who else would put gas in my car for me? Dennis didn't usually help me out, but there was a first time for everything.

The television was loud again and the apartment had a weird musty smell. I sniffed the air, trying to pin down the stench when my eyes began to water.

"Have you been smoking?" I asked, angrily.

"Don't worry, it wasn't in your precious apartment," he said. "I went outside."

His eyes didn't move from the TV screen. I wanted to scream at him for smoking in my apartment, but I didn't want to ruin the one good thing he did.

"Thanks for putting gas in my car," I said as I leaned into his line of sight.

He gave me an annoyed look, then looked back at the screen.

"Where's my sandwich?" he asked.

Guilt filled me, making my stomach drop. I felt so bad about forgetting the sandwich, I forgot about everything else. Dennis had the ability to make me feel horrible about simple mistakes.

"Oh no, I completely forgot," I said.

"You were right there."

"I know, I'm so sorry," I said. "Do you want me to make something for you?"

"You don't have anything. I already checked," he said. "Maybe we can go get something once this game is over."

"I can't. I have to work tonight."

"You call that work? You just like rubbing elbows with those fancy people."

"I like doing the events. Plus I need that money to pay for grad school."

And to keep you comfy on my couch apparently.

"Well, you work a lot," he said. "More than I ever did and I made more than you. You should really consider whether it's worth your time or not."

"Worth my time?" I stared at him for a minute. After all this time, how could he not understand how much I enjoyed working these events? It kept me busy which meant I didn't have time to think about all the things that were wrong in my life, like having an ex-boyfriend who kept staying with me.

"I think once I get promoted, you should think about this more," he said. "Figure out how much you're making waitressing for Samantha and if it's really worth your time. You could move in with me and just focus on going to school."

What???

I couldn't deal with him anymore. Dennis was an accountant at a big firm. He was very proud of that fact and how much money he made. I wondered how he was able to function in such a high profile, high stress environment when the Dennis I knew melted down putting together IKEA furniture.

I stared at him as I tried to figure out what was going on in his head, but he just turned back to the game. Did he really think that was a good idea? Did he think we were still together? Had he completely lost his mind?

Shaking my head, I walked out of the living room and into my bedroom. The last thing I wanted to do was get into another fight. I only had to put up with him for three more days and then he'd be gone. At least that's what I hoped.

Chapter Four

Jackie

The next day, I rushed home from class and quickly changed into my nicer pair of jeans and a purple knit top. Dennis was looking through the cupboards in the kitchen when I came out of my room.

"Where are you going?" he asked.

"Samantha invited me for dinner," I said.

"And you're not inviting me to come along? Don't you think that's rude?"

"I think it's rude of you to expect an invitation. And I think it's rude that you're going through my cupboards when you haven't given me money for groceries. When is your apartment going to be ready?"

"If you don't want me here just say so and I'll sleep in the car or something," he said

"You don't even have a car. Do you really think I'd let you sleep in my car?"

"I don't need a car. Work gives me a rental when I travel which is a lot. You're being a real bitch, you know that?"

I held myself back from blowing up at him. It wouldn't help and I'd only end up late for dinner. In my head I counted backwards from ten as I grabbed my bag and walked out the door.

I'll deal with him another time.

***

As I waited outside, Samantha came down the steps and waved to me. She had a baby monitor in her other hand. When she opened the door, I couldn't keep my mouth shut.

"You realize this is the last place I want to be, right?" I said, entering as I removed my sweater.

Samantha took my sweater and hung it in the dreaded coat closet. I couldn't even look at that closet without thinking about Brent.

She rolled her eyes.

"I don't know what it is with the two of you," she said. "I saw the two of you at my wedding and I know you both probably better than anyone. I'm telling you, you're perfect for each other. And since nothing is going on between the two of you, I'm taking matters into my own hands."

"By forcing us to eat together? You know what happened last time."

"One cannot think well, love well, sleep well, if one has not dined well," she said.

"You realize it's unfair to quote Virginia Woolf," I said.

"What can I say, I fight dirty."

As we entered the kitchen, Sam checked on the roast in the oven.

"You've been really pushing for me and Brent even more lately. I think having that baby has done something to your brain," I said.

"It has. It's made me realize how Drake and I could've been together even longer. I wasted time away from him when I could have been happy instead. I want that happiness for you."

I appreciated that Sam was looking out for my happiness, but I didn't understand why she just wouldn't listen to me.

"I've told you, I don't need it and I don't want it," I said. "Look, just because you're in a state of matrimonial bliss, that doesn't mean everyone else needs it. We've had this talk before. You know I don't want to get married."

Sam grimaced as she folded her arms in front of her.

"It's me you're talking to," she said. "I know you, Jackie. Just like I know how hard my wedding was on you."

"It wasn't."

"You're one of my best friends, Jackie. I *know*. I was there that day, remember?"

Remember? That was a day I've been trying to forget for five years. Somehow it still felt like just yesterday.

"Listen, Sam. You know I love you. You know I was honored to be your maid of honor," I said. "And it was a beautiful wedding. Even if it was on the beach."

"I'm sorry about the beach. I know that made it harder on you."

I sighed. "I'm a big girl, Sam. What happened with Marc was a long time ago."

"Have you ever cried about it? I mean, even that day I don't remember you crying."

"No. I haven't and I'm not going to. Marc doesn't deserve my tears. Now can we talk about something else?"

"Sorry," she said quietly.

"It's okay," I said as I hugged her. "I know you're just looking out for me. Now seriously, please, let's talk about something else. Anything else."

"Anything? How about Brent?"

"Really?" I asked, a little surprised.

"Too soon? I'll have to remember to bring him up again later after he's gone," she said with an evil grin

"Where is he anyway?"

"His meeting went long so he take another flight back. The car service should be dropping him off any minute."

"Yeah right," I said. "Maybe he's picking up Brandi."

"He's not like that. I don't know why you think he is. That night at dinner was…I don't know what it was, but he's not like that."

"He's just like Marc," I said. "On the outside he seems like a nice guy. He's got a great dog, he's got a great job that actually does something good, and he's hot. But, on the inside, he's a shitty person."

"No he's not, Jackie. I know him."

"Then you're just falling for it."

"He's a really great guy. I swear he is. I don't know why you think he's not."

"He didn't call," I blurted out and immediately regretted it. The reason I hated Brent sounded even more ridiculous and immature when I said it aloud.

"You have to get over that," she said.

I put my hand up. "Before you go on about how you're sure he has a perfectly simple explanation for that, you have to hear me out." I paused and she nodded. "He said he would call and he didn't. I know what's next. There's always something else. A meeting that went late, a car that needs repair, a family member who suddenly needs something. There's always an excuse to not keep his word."

My relationship with Marc flashed through my head. All the excuses, all the reasons he couldn't be there for me, everything was never his fault. At the time, I didn't realize any of that and even after we broke up I repeated a lot of my mistakes by replacing Marc with Dennis.

Marc was like a scab that wouldn't heal. Every so often I would be reminded of something he did or said and the scab would open. No matter what I did, I couldn't get over him. It didn't matter that I didn't love him anymore, all that hurt was still there because I kept stuffing it away. I didn't want to deal with it.

"He's not like that," she said softly.

"Do you know how many times I said that about Marc? I can't go through that again. And I'm done talking about this."

I walked out of the kitchen and onto the back patio. If I had enough balls I would have left.

"I'm sorry," Samantha called out behind me.

I wasn't angry with Sam. Her heart was in the right place. I just wished she would butt out sometimes.

A cool breeze came off the ocean. In the distance a boat's lights blinked on the water. I walked to the edge of the patio, to where the sand started, and stared out into the darkness.

"Normally I'd complain about my view being blocked, but I think it just got better," Brent said from behind me.

You've got to be kidding me, I thought.

I spun around and found him sitting down, his long legs crossed at the knee.

"I'll just head inside," I said. "It's too cold out here anyway."

"I've been thinking about you," he said.

"Oh? What about me?" I asked, preparing myself for a sarcastic comment.

"You're not heading in?" he teased. "I thought you were cold."

"I guess I'm more curious than cold," I said.

He stood up and removed his suit jacket. With his jacket in one hand, he used the other to beckon me to him.

I walked over to him and as he slipped the jacket over my shoulders, he whispered in my ear.

"I've been thinking about how much I enjoyed kissing you."

I turned around and eyed him suspiciously, waiting for the punch line that didn't come.

"What do you want?" I asked.

He laughed. "I don't know what you're talking about. But now that I think about it, you do owe me, you know."

"I owe you?"

"How quickly we forget." Brent put his hands in his pockets and rocked confidently on his heels. "I came to your rescue the other day, remember? You were a damsel in distress and I gave you a ride you'll never forget."

"Hmm...technically, since I drove, doesn't that mean I gave you a ride?"

"It was my car. Besides, when I say I gave you a ride, I really mean something else." He wiggled his brow lasciviously.

"See, that right there. That's why I never believe anything you say. Everything is just a joke to you. You just say whatever you can to get what you want."

"If that's true then it hasn't worked very well for me," he said.

"What makes you say that?"

"I haven't had you in my bed," he said. "Yet."

"Yet? You sound pretty confident for a man who keeps getting turned down."

"Well, like I said before, you owe me. And I am feeling pretty confident. You see, I know you keep saying that you can't stand me, but after that kiss the other day I think you've been lying."

"And what about you?" I asked. "Every time I see you, you're teasing me about something. It's pretty obvious to me that you don't like me just as much as I don't like you."

"Then there's no reason why you won't agree to this. I have a proposition for you."

"A proposition? I thought you said I owe you."

"You do, but it's much more fun if you agree to it because you want to and not just because I say so," he said.

Fun? What on earth is he thinking about?

"Well, you definitely have me curious," I said.

"Before I tell you about it, you have to first admit something to me," he said.

"Admit something? What?" I asked, confused.

Brent leaned closer to me. He smelled like warm spice, which always comforted me.

"Admit that you enjoyed that kiss the other day. I won't even bring up what happened in the coat closet at the wedding, even though I really want to."

My cheeks burned as I thought about that kiss and everything else. I would never admit to him how much I loved kissing him.

"No? Maybe you need a reminder," he said.

His lips touched mine and wanting more, I parted my lips without thinking.

"It's alright, you don't have to say anything," he said. "Your lips give you away. I know you hate me, but you can't deny what you're feeling right now."

He slipped his hand into the back of my hair and kissed me again. This time he didn't stop as we kissed hungrily.

I forced myself to push him away, but it was a half-hearted attempt.

"What does that have to do with anything?" I asked feeling breathless.

"Like I said, I've been doing a lot of thinking. If kissing you feels this good, imagine what everything else would be like."

"Oh, so that's your proposition? Sex?" I asked. "You seem to forget that we hate each other."

"If I just wanted sex, I could get that from anyone. But there's something about you, Jackie. We don't have to like each other to sleep together. If you want to still hate me while I make you orgasm, then that's up to you." He grinned as he cocked his brow at me, then slipped his business card into my hand. "Take some time to think about it."

Think about it? All I've been doing since the wedding has been thinking about it.

"Wait," I said as I caught up to him.

I grabbed his shoulder and he turned towards me. He pushed me against the wall as he kissed me again and pressed his body to mine. He kissed my forehead before he stepped back.

"Think about it. You know how to reach me," he said as he turned and left.

Chapter Five

Brent

"You seem to forget that we hate each other," Jackie said

Her words echoed in my head as we kissed.

Why does she think I hate her?

I couldn't keep kissing her. If my lips touched her plump lips again I would have no choice but to carry her inside the house and rip her clothes off. I had to leave.

"Think about it," I said as I pulled away. "You know how to reach me."

I entered the house and saw Sam setting the table. I'd have to make it up to Samantha, but I knew she'd understand. Despite how much she kept wanting to get Jackie and I together, I knew it wasn't meant to be. I knew something that Sam didn't—Jackie belonged to someone else.

As I reached the front door, I glanced over my shoulder. Jackie was leaning against the wall, still wearing my suit jacket. Her hair was a little messy and her cheeks were still flushed. I wondered if she needed the wall to keep her upright. I grinned at the thought, feeling the same way.

It wasn't right though. She infuriated me. Where was he? Where was this guy? How come I never saw them together?

I quickly texted an apology to Sam as I got into my car. Jackie had been haunting me since the wedding. Despite the knowledge that she was involved with someone else, I couldn't stop thinking about her. Every ounce of my being said she was mine.

Once I got onto the freeway, I called my friend Gunnar Craven. Gunnar and I were roommates in college. Lately we had been working together as I tried to spread awareness for environmental protection. Gunnar was one of the heads of a large advertising agency in New York City and he was convinced that he could make people interested in saving the environment.

"Hey, Brent," Gunnar said as he answered the phone. "Where are you?"

In the background I heard a woman giggle and the mixture of music and people talking. Gunnar was always at a party, bar, or restaurant.

"I'm in the car," I said. "I just left Sam and Drake's."

"Weren't you having dinner there tonight? Did something happen? You sound like you need a drink."

"Actually, yeah, I could. Where are you?"

"That new bar downtown."

"Pivot?"

"Yeah, that's it."

"Alright, I'm on my way."

***

Pivot was an ultra-modern bar with a sleek monochromatic style. When I arrived, Gunnar was surrounded by several women in a circular booth. He used to joke that he majored in satisfying women back in school, but I always suspected he went through so many women because he was looking for someone really special.

He ordered a couple of beers for us and as the waitress delivered them, he held his hands up to get everyone's attention.

"Now ladies, you know I would love nothing more than to sit and talk to you, but right now my buddy needs me." He caught the waitress's attention before she left the table. "These ladies won't be paying for their drinks tonight."

As the ladies left, I slid into the booth and took a drink from my frosted mug.

"Don't you ever get tired of this?" I asked.

"Of what?" Gunnar asked. "The women? Never."

"No, the bar scene."

"This is all research. They talk about the things they like, and I listen. I figure out what draws them to their purchases and then I can market to them better. These women are where the money is. The fact that I get to please them in bed is just the icing on the cake. But who gives a fuck about me, what's going on with you? You look like someone stole your blanket."

"I don't know," I said. "There's this girl."

"It's always about a girl."

"She hates me, but when we kiss I know there's something there. I know she should be mine."

"So then make her yours," he said.

"She's with someone else," I grunted. "I don't get it, because Sam is always saying we'd be perfect together and they're pretty tight, but Sam seems to think Jackie is single."

"Maybe she is single."

"No, she's not. I spoke to her boyfriend."

"When?"

"A while back. After Sam and Drake's wedding," I said. "She gave me her number and I called that night. Her boyfriend answered and said it's a game she likes to play. She gives guys her number for the fun of it."

"That doesn't sound like the kind of woman you're usually into."

"Honestly, I didn't think she was like that," I said. "But he answered her phone and it was pretty late. If he wasn't her boyfriend, then what was he doing there?"

"I'm sorry. Maybe it's better if you move on from this one."

I shook my head. "I can't. I've been trying to and I end up obsessing about her even more. It's like I've become a crazy person."

"So then what the hell? Go for it. What do you have to lose?"

What did I have to lose?

I thought about the proposition I made to Jackie earlier. I didn't really mean anything by it. I was drunk off her lips when I suggested it. I didn't think she would entertain the idea at all, but if she did maybe it meant something.

Maybe I was wrong in thinking she had a boyfriend. Sam should know and she didn't think so. So what if this guy said she was his girl and they had a future together? I didn't know him and Jackie wasn't the kind of girl to two-time anyone. What if Dennis lied to me?

Whatever the truth was about how she felt about me, she couldn't deny that kiss.

Taking my phone out, I set it on the table and thought about what to say. I thought about what she said earlier about being curious and how her body melted against mine whenever we kissed. I had made a ridiculous offer to her before, and I had nothing to lose.

Sam had given me Jackie's cell number weeks ago, but I never called her. I wasn't going to call a woman who made it a habit to remind me of her hatred. But tonight was different.

I saw something in her eyes that made me want to take a risk. I saw something that said I had a chance.

"Brent?" Jackie said as she answered the phone.

It didn't slip past me that she must have added me to her contacts. It made me even more confident in my plan. I would make Jackie mine some way, somehow.

"About my proposition earlier," I said. "Forget you hate me for just one night. That's all I'm asking for."

Chapter Six

Jackie

After Brent left, I couldn't stay at Samantha's for dinner. I knew what would happen, Sam would keep going on and on about how wonderful her brother-in-law was. I didn't want to hear about it. The last thing I wanted to do was talk about Brent Winslow.

I needed to get home. I wanted to grab that container of cookie dough ice cream I just bought and think about what he said. Was he serious? Was he playing games with my head? What did he mean?

My mind spun as I tried to figure out what he meant or if it was all a joke.

As I entered my apartment, I was grateful that Dennis was out instead of planted on the couch like always. I headed straight to the refrigerator, pulled out the carton of Haagen Dazs, grabbed a spoon, and sat down at the small kitchen table.

Scooping a large spoonful, I sighed as I took a taste. With the spoon stuck in my mouth, I pulled my phone out of my bag with Brent's business card. Winslow Environmental was a few blocks away from my school, but I never pieced together that it was Brent's company.

Flipping his card over, I saw he wrote his cell on the back. Without thinking, I added his number into my contacts list.

Maybe I should call him, I thought. *How else will I know for sure what he meant?*

My phone buzzed as Brent's number lit up my screen. Oh no. Did I accidentally call him? What do I do? Should I answer? I have to answer.

"Brent?" I said as I answered.

"About my proposition earlier," Brent said. "Forget you hate me for just one night. That's all I'm asking for."

I stared at the phone for a moment, wondering if I was imagining this. Did the man I hate just ask me to spend the night with him? And if I hate him so much, why do I want to so badly?

"Are you serious?" I asked.

"Dead serious. One night, you and me. All night. I can't promise you'll get much sleep, but maybe you'll change your mind about me."

There was that confidence again. I couldn't deny that no matter how much I wanted to keep disliking him, it was damn near impossible.

"I'll think about it," I said, glad he wasn't there to see the smile on my face.

***

I spent the next few days finding that everything reminded me of Brent. I wanted to call or text him and just say yes, but then I started wondering what kind of girl did that make me?

Did I just want to have one night with Brent? Definitely not. That wasn't who I was, but it wasn't who I thought he was either. Samantha was too much of his cheerleader for him to be some kind of manwhore. I couldn't help but think that his proposition meant something else, but I had been wrong before. Thinking about my track record, I wasn't the best in picking men.

He didn't call when he said he would and now he wants a one-night-stand. Sounds perfect! I thought.

No wonder I was so attracted to Brent. He fit my wrong guy bill perfectly.

Already dressed in my black slacks, white button-down shirt, and black tie, I was ready for work but had a few minutes before I had to leave. Dennis was sitting on the couch in his usual spot, watching a football game.

As much as we clashed, I had to admit I liked having Dennis around. I didn't like living by myself.

During a commercial, Dennis muted the television, then got up to go to the kitchen.

"Do you want anything?" he asked.

"No, thanks," I said. "I'll be leaving soon. Do you have any plans for tonight?"

"Yeah, watching the rest of this game. I have some money on it." He opened a can of Coke and took a long sip as he looked at me. "You do something different?"

I looked down at myself, then smoothed my ponytail, expecting him to criticize me. As far as I could tell, everything was fine.

"No, what's wrong?" I asked.

"Nothing's wrong. You look good, happy." He shrugged. "I don't know." He sat back on the couch, but closer to me than usual. "I miss you," he said softly.

Huh?

"How can you miss me? You see me every day."

"That's not what I meant," he said as he moved closer to me.

He had that look in his eye that I recognized as his come hither, sexy time look. I hadn't seen it since we last dated over a year ago. I moved a couple inches away from him, hoping he'd get the hint, but instead he tilted his head towards me with his lips pursed and his eyes closed like a sick guppy.

"What are you doing?" I pushed him away and stood up.

"What? You gave me that look," he said.

"I gave you no such look! Get that out of your head right now. We are completely and totally platonic. You know that."

"I'm sorry, okay? It'll never happen again."

"It better not," I said as I grabbed my bag. "Have you heard anything about your apartment?"

"I spoke to the landlord yesterday. He said just another couple of days, so don't worry, I know when I'm not wanted. I'll be out of your hair soon."

Grrrrr! I don't have time for this bullshit.

I left without saying another word. It was the perfect reminder of how bad I was with picking boyfriends. I pushed all thoughts of Brent into the back of my mind. At least at work I'd be too busy to think about him.

Chapter Seven

Jackie

That night I was working a big event at the Arc Hotel, one of the largest hotels in Canyon Cove. Usually I knew everything about the events I worked at, especially since I started working for Samantha, but this one was different.

Tonight was extra important for Samantha since it was a new client, a big advertising agency she had been trying to get some catering work from for a long time. Since she was home with the baby, I told her I would manage the cooking and wait staff to make sure everything turned out perfectly.

I had just finished going over everything on my clipboard when the guests started to arrive. Standing next to the bar was a tall man with short dark hair and beard. He was model handsome and in his perfectly tailored suit, he could have stepped out of GQ magazine. I knew right away he was the client.

"Mr. Craven, right?" I asked.

He turned to look at me, gave me a once over and smiled.

"Definitely," he said. "But please call me Gunnar."

"I'm Jackie Stone--"

"Ahh, yes, now I get it. You've got that sweet, sexy thing going on."

"Excuse me?"

"Don't play coy with me," he said. "You're one of those who on the outside is proper and sweet, but I bet you're a wild one in the sack."

In the restaurant and food service world, I was used to my fair share of sexual harassment, but this was a little overboard.

"That's really inappropriate," I said.

"See, that's exactly what I'm talking about." He laughed as he rubbed his chin, looking satisfied. "It's no wonder he can't stop thinking about you."

"Wait, what did you just say?" I asked.

A loud crash echoed through the room.

Shoot! What was that?

"Hold that thought," I said. "I'll be back."

I rushed over and found one of the waitresses trying to clean up the mess from an overturned cart. The floor was covered with plates, some which had shattered from the impact.

"What happened?" I asked.

"I'm sorry, Miss Stone," she said. "The wheel caught and I gave the cart a good push to unstick it, but it fell over."

I waved another member of the wait staff over and told them to hurry and clean up the mess, thankful it wasn't the food. As I surveyed the room, everything else looked fine.

Glancing back at the bar to keep an eye on where Gunnar was, I noticed he wasn't alone anymore. Standing beside him was another perfectly tailored suit with broad shoulders, but this man had blond hair. I didn't need to see his face to recognize Brent.

Seriously, how is he everywhere now?

Maybe Samantha was right, maybe fate was throwing us together, but I refused to believe that. This was Samantha's job and it wouldn't surprise me if she told Brent I would be here. But why was he talking to Gunnar? Could Brent be the guy Gunnar was talking about?

As I started making my way over to the bar, Brent met me halfway.

"I heard you met Gunnar," he said.

"I did. And he said some interesting things," I said.

"He has a way with words." Brent's hand touched my back softly. "Can I talk to you privately?"

"Sure, I need to make sure everything has left the kitchen anyway."

As we entered the empty kitchen, Brent pushed me against the wall and kissed me. I dropped the clipboard and pulled him closer to me. I didn't care that he didn't call or about my bad decisions, I just wanted him.

Chapter Eight

Jackie

Brent picked me up as we kissed and I wrapped my legs around him. I tilted my head back as his lips brushed against my neck.

"When do you get off work?" he asked, his voice husky.

"When the night is over," I said.

"Then I'll tell everyone to leave now."

"Samantha would kill you."

"How do you think she got this job? Gunnar's a good friend."

He pressed his body against me as he bit my earlobe.

"Is it true you can't stop thinking about me?" I asked.

"I told you he talks too much," Brent said. "But I did tell you that the other day."

"No, you said you had been thinking about me. You didn't say you couldn't stop."

"I can't stop. I don't want to stop," he said, then kissed me again. "Come home with me tonight."

Yes!

"No," I said, wondering what was wrong with me. "I don't...I mean...you and I..."

I didn't know what I was trying to say. Everything in my head screamed, "Yes, yes, go home with him!" But my mouth said something different.

Brent set me down and his eyes darkened, making them almost black. He clenched his jaw tightly as he shoved his hands into his pockets.

"Forget you hate me for just one night," he said.

I wanted to tell him I didn't hate him. That I was a stupid person dealing with baggage I couldn't get over and that he'd be better off running in the other direction, but none of that came out of my mouth.

"Just one night?" I asked.

"Just one," he said as he turned away from me. "It won't mean anything. It'll just be two adults having fun. And when morning comes you can go back to hating me and pretend none of this happened."

He sounded so cold, so unemotional. It wasn't like him.

"Is that what you really want?" I asked.

He looked over his shoulder at me and our eyes met.

"What do you want? What do you really want?" he asked.

What did I want? I wished I knew the answer. Right there and then all I wanted was to be with him. And I didn't care if it was only one night.

"Meet me here at midnight," I said.

***

I was in the middle of wiping down the kitchen when I heard the echo of Brent's shoes on the floor. I had rushed to finish everything up as soon as all the guests left, hoping to be done before midnight. The result was that my hair had fallen out of my ponytail. I was a mess.

I pulled the elastic from my hair and shook my hair loose. As I gathered my hair back, Brent came up behind me, took the elastic from my hands, and wrapped his arms around my waist.

"I'm sorry about before," he whispered. "It's no wonder you hate me."

He kissed my neck and even though I didn't want him to stop, I couldn't help how gross I felt.

"No," I said. "I don't think this is going to work out tonight. I was being impulsive before when I said yes."

Brent's head bobbed slowly.

"I can understand that," he said. "I can be impulsive too. I don't want you to regret anything."

"It's not that," I said. "I don't think I'd regret it at all, it's just...I'm a mess. The kitchen is hot back here. I'm sweaty and really need a shower."

"Today's your lucky day. I just so happen to have a shower at my house. I'd be happy to let you use mine."

I thought about his offer and as much as part of me wanted to say no and keep hating him, a bigger part of me wanted him.

"You sure?" I asked.

"You know how long I've wanted you?"

I shook my head.

"I'm going to make you come so much, you'll forget everyone else you were with," he said with a lopsided grin.

"Oh? You're going to make me a virgin again?"

His laugh echoed through the kitchen.

"Just come home with me," he said. "Like I said before, give me one night. If you don't want to see me again after that, then I'll back off, but I'm hoping after I make you come five or six times that you might hate me a little less."

"Five or six times? I'm going to hold you to that, you know," I said.

"I'll keep count for you."

***

We left my car at the hotel. Brent had a Maserati like the one he donated to charity, but this one was white.

I shifted in my seat to look at him while he drove. I still thought he could substitute for Ken if Barbie ever needed a date, but there was something more to him than just being gorgeous.

"It's weird," I said. "I feel like I've known you for so long, but I really don't know much about you."

"There isn't much to know about me," he said as he turned off the freeway. "But I know what you mean. From the first moment I saw you I felt connected to you somehow."

"Maybe it's because we're both so close to Samantha."

"That could be it."

He glanced at me out of the corner of his eye and smiled.

"What do you want to know?" he asked.

I thought about his question as we drove past a golf course. I knew he grew up in Canyon Cove and I knew he was a big time attorney who worked to protect the environment and various charities. The more I thought about it the more I realized I did know a lot about him, except for one thing.

"How come you stayed in Canyon Cove?" I asked.

"Actually I didn't. After I got my law degree I moved to New York City for a while. I lived there until about a year ago when I decided to move back."

"Is that why you're so close to Gunnar?"

"He and I have been friends a long time. When I got to New York, I used to join him and his other ad friends going to the bar and picking up women. I'm almost embarrassed to admit it was like a sport for us."

"Why did you stop?" I asked.

"Because that wasn't me. We had a lot of fun for a while, but eventually it didn't matter to me. I realized I wanted more."

"Is that when you moved back?"

"No, that's when I met Bryn. Bryn and I connected right away. She was an attorney at another law firm. She was smart, beautiful, and I didn't know it at the time, but she was taken." Brent's face hardened. "I guess I have a type," he muttered.

"What do you mean?"

He cleared his throat.

"Never mind," he said. "Bryn told me she was in a loveless relationship. She said they had been together for a long time but never broke up because it was easier to keep things as they were.

She said he had other women and she had me. It wasn't what I wanted though, I wanted a relationship. By the time she told me about her relationship, I had already fallen in love."

I thought about my own bad relationships and how sometimes love made a person do things they wouldn't normally do.

"I tried to keep the relationship the way it was. Bryn made it easy to forget she was with someone else. She never spoke about him, she was free to see me whenever I wanted, every thing was great as long as I didn't think about the truth," he said.

"So what happened?"

"I was out one night with Gunnar and the guys. We were out celebrating when the man at a nearby table proposed. They were passing out champagne to celebrate and that's when I saw the woman was Bryn. She was radiant and happy wearing the ring he just gave her. I couldn't pretend anymore." Brent silently steered up a small hill. "I decided New York wasn't all it was cracked up to be so I started my own practice here in Canyon Cove."

"Do you ever think about her?"

"No, not really," he said. "Honestly I question whether I really loved her or if it was just some childish crush. I learned a lot from it though."

Brent stopped his car in front of a set of wide gates. A guard stepped out from the building to get a better look, then waved to Brent as he pressed the button to open the gates.

I had heard about the Canyon Coast section before, but never knew anyone who had been there. Canyon Coast was a small group of mansions on the top of a hill that overlooked the ocean.

The houses didn't look like anything spectacular from the street, but I had heard what made these homes special was their view.

Brent pulled into a driveway that sloped down behind a Craftsman style home. The underground garage opened as we approached and inside Brent had a collection of exotic cars. The garage was big enough to house three of my apartments.

As we got out of the car, Brent held his hand out to me.

"Come, I'm sure you want that shower," he said as we entered the house.

Shade was waiting as we entered the house. His tail wagged with such force, his entire body wiggled. I knelt down to say hello to him and he knocked me over as he excitedly rubbed his head against me.

"Shade, I've told you before, a little wine and some dinner and then you can knock them over," Brent said.

"I guess he's used to you having a lot of women over?" I asked, trying to keep my jealousy in check.

"No, not unless you count family. I told you, I'm not that guy."

I wanted to believe him, but in the back of my mind I kept thinking about his proposition. Why else would he want me there if he wasn't that guy? He was the one who said it was only for one night.

Brent led me through the house and upstairs to a large bedroom that faced the back of the house. The wall was all glass and even though it was dark, I could make out the lights of a couple of small fishing boats on the water.

I followed Brent into the bathroom and couldn't believe how huge it was. The shower was it's own room. It had several shower heads on the walls and each one had a line of jets underneath it. Just outside the open doorway for the shower was a control box for steam and to control the jet spray.

"Wow," I said. "You weren't kidding when you said you had a shower."

He smiled and pulled me against him.

"Mind if I join you?" he asked, his voice husky.

My heart pounded in my chest. It had been so long since I was with anyone, I was afraid I'd explode on first contact. I bit my lip and swallowed nervously as he turned the shower on.

Brent undressed me slowly. Peeling each layer of clothing off as he gently caressed my body. I entered the shower and let the warm water run over my skin as I watched him take his clothes off.

His shoulders rippled as he removed his shirt, exposing his perfect abs. I could have stared at his stomach muscles all day, but once he was completely naked my eyes moved to his stiff manhood.

Brent entered the shower and his hands immediately cupped my face, pulling me up to his lips. His tongue slipped against mine before he pulled away and grinned.

"You wanted a shower first," he said as a smile tugged at his lips.

He reached for the soap and lathered it up in his hands. His strong hands moved over my body as he bathed me. As the water rinsed the soap from my skin, his mouth claimed the spot. I was getting dizzy between the combination of his smooth hands with the hunger of his lips.

I wondered if he was secretly torturing me and getting back at me for hating him so much. But if this was my punishment, I would keep doing the crime.

Once he was done with the soap, he kissed me hungrily. I held onto his slick skin as the jets of the shower burst against us.

"This is one," he said as our eyes met.

"One?"

"I told you I would keep count."

His lips slipped over my neck and down my collar bone as his hands grasped my ass firmly. He lowered himself, kissing me as he went, until he was kneeling in front of me.

Gingerly he lifted my leg, as his fingers moved over my sex. His smiled slyly as I leaned against the shower wall.

He kissed my inner thigh and then sucked where it met the rest of my body. I giggled and his eyes darted up before his lips moved closer to my sex.

His tongue slipped over my clit and I moaned. I knew it would be fast for me since it had been so long. I reached for the wall, afraid I was going to fall as my core throbbed.

"Please, Brent, I'm so close," I said.

He stood up, holding my thigh in his hand. Drops of water sliding down his face.

"This is still one," he said.

His cock pressed against my entrance, teasing me at first. I wrapped my arms around his shoulders, pressing my breasts against him as he entered me.

I was so close before that feeling him inside me, pushed me over. Chills shot through my body as my orgasm crashed over me. Brent held me tight as my body writhed against him.

I threw my head back as I caught my breath and Brent kissed my throat before our mouths met. I wanted more.

"Ready for two?" he asked.

"Yes."

Chapter Nine

Jackie

The sun streaming through the windows woke me. I didn't know what to think about what happened between us. Last night had been the most amazing sex I ever had. It was even better than what Brent had hinted things between us could be like. But now that morning was here, things had to go back to the way they were.

Brent's arms were still around me as we spooned. I didn't want to wake him so I carefully rolled onto my back, but he was already awake.

"Still hate me?" he asked.

"Yes," I said, fighting back a smile.

"Oh well, I tried."

He kissed my lips tenderly.

"Did you sleep alright?" he asked.

He kissed my forehead softly, then smiled.

"Yes," I said. "Did you?"

"I didn't sleep," he said. "I was watching you. You're beautiful when you're asleep."

"Only when I'm asleep?"

"You're beautiful all the time, but there's something about when you're sleeping that makes you look angelic." He brushed my hair off my cheek. "It's probably the lack of that line etched between your brows."

"What are you talking about?"

I rubbed the spot between my brows, trying to feel what he was talking about.

"It's your angry look," he said. "Whenever you're angry or upset, you get that line. It's a nice reminder of how you feel about me."

"Oh, well, I'm sorry about that," I said.

"No, you're entitled to your feelings."

I sat up and pulled the sheets around me to cover my naked body. I wanted to explain to him why I treated him the way I did, but I couldn't figure out what had changed. Why didn't I hate him anymore? Was I making another bad choice?

Pulling the sheet with me, I got out of bed and started picking up my clothes.

"What are you doing?" he asked.

"You said this was done when morning came."

"Right," he said.

He got out of bed and I could tell something had changed in him from just before. He was quiet and cold again like he was in the kitchen. I didn't understand what was going on. Did I do something wrong? I was only following his rules.

"I need you to drive me back to the Arc so I can get my car," I said.

He nodded, then disappeared through a door. The shower started and I peeked in to watch the water roll down his golden skin. I stayed in the doorway, watching his reflection in the mirror until the steam clouded my view.

When he was dressed, he walked past me almost like I wasn't there.

"Let's go," he said.

We drove in silence. I kept thinking about everything that happened the night before and I wondered what I did wrong.

He parked next to my car and I hesitated a moment wondering if I should say something, but I didn't know what. As I opened the car door, he reached for my hand.

"Can I see you again?" he asked.

His eyes glowed with affection which confused me more.

"I thought it was just for one night," I said.

Please tell me I'm wrong, I thought. *Say something, Brent, anything,* I silently begged.

"Just for sex," he said as he looked away. "I promise you can keep hating me."

Chapter Ten

Brent

Jackie left my car in a huff with that line between her brows screaming at me. She had no place to be mad. I wasn't the one in a relationship. If she wanted something more, I needed to know that guy she was living with was history.

As she drove away, I checked my phone and saw a text from Gunnar.

Gunnar: Did you take her home?
Brent: Yes, but she's already gone.

Gunnar's name flitted across the screen as my phone rang.

"What are you doing up so early?" I asked.

"I'm always up this early," he said. "I've got to do my strut of pride on my way home. I guess that's what Jackie is doing too."

"It's complicated," I said.

"Complicated sometimes makes the sex even better," he said.

"I'm not talking to you about that. I just need to figure out how to win her over."

"Did you ever find out why she hates you?" Gunnar asked. "What did you do?"

"I didn't do anything," I said.

"Come on, be a man and own that shit. If a woman hates you, you damn well know you did something wrong."

"That's the thing, I really don't know. We had a great time at my brother's wedding and then when I called her, her boyfriend answered the phone."

"Boyfriend? You sure? Shit, that sucks. She doesn't seem the type though, man."

"I know, that's what's confusing as hell. I don't get it and part of me wonders if that douche was lying to me when he said that," I said.

"And what about last night? She say anything about the boyfriend?" he asked.

"I didn't ask, she didn't tell," I said. "As much as this sucks, I'll take whatever I can get as long as I get some time with her."

"Just fucking ask her, man. Ask her if she has a boyfriend."

I shook my head. There was no way Gunnar would ever understand how I felt about her. If I knew for a fact that she had a boyfriend, it would kill me.

"I don't want to hear her say she does," I said.

"You really are a pussy. You know that, right?" Gunnar said.

"Fuck you, man," I said with a laugh.

"Not in a million years," he said.

***

A week had passed since I had last seen Jackie, but all I did was think about her. Her sweet vanilla scent still hung in the air of my bedroom, and when I closed my eyes I could imagine the warmth of her body against mine.

I was worse than a lovesick puppy.

I spent the past week trying to drown myself in work. I was in the middle of looking over some ideas Gunnar had for ads when my secretary, Marcia, knocked on the office door and set a piece of paper on my desk.

"There's the list for this week," Marcia said as she left. "Also, it's almost one o'clock."

"Thank you, Marcia," I said.

With my eyes still on the computer, I slid the paper over and then looked at the list. For months now my secretary had been giving me a list of the events Jackie was working at. Between Marcia and Samantha I knew what Jackie was up to almost every day of the week.

I wasn't proud of it, but I couldn't sit around and wait for Samantha's dinners to see Jackie. I needed to see her as often as possible.

I packed up my laptop and left my office. I had less than twenty minutes to make it to the Canyon Cove University campus for the end of class. After not seeing Jackie in so long, I looked forward to the walk and accidentally running into her.

Students were filing out of the angular building as I arrived. I leaned against the stone wall across from the entry and waited for her. As she walked out of the building, the sun made her hair glossy and luminous. Even with her worn yoga pants and oversized sweatshirt, I still thought she was breathtaking.

She smiled as she approached, and the line between her eyebrows was gone.

"What are you doing here?" she asked.

"Waiting for you," I said. "How about dinner tonight?"

"Dinner? You mean like a date? What about the rules? You know, our arrangement."

Her phone started ringing before I could respond. She answered the phone, and while I should have stepped away to give her privacy, as soon as I heard her answer it, I knew I was staying.

"What is it, Dennis?" she said as she answered the phone.

Her face grew pale as her mouth slacked open. As she looked at me, her eyes welled up with tears. I was ready to grab the phone from her and tear Dennis a new one for making her so upset.

"Totaled?" she said into the phone, her voice rising. "Why didn't you stop?"

"Is that all you care about? That fucking piece of shit car? It was old and only worked half the time anyway. You didn't even ask if I was okay," he yelled loud enough that I could hear him through the phone.

"I...I'm sorry," she stammered, her brow furrowed. "You didn't say you were in the hospital. I didn't think...I'm sorry."

"I'm fine," he yelled. "Luckily your goddamn car was so fucking huge that it protected me. Now I have to figure out how to get back home. Why does this shit always happen to me?"

I grabbed the phone from her hand, hung up on Dennis, then tossed it aside. As Jackie fought back tears, I put my arm around her shoulders and brought her closer to me. She cried against my chest as I held her.

Who the hell did this guy think he was? That wasn't how a real man talked to a woman. Why did Jackie put up with it?

I had so many questions for her, the biggest being why she was still with him, but asking her about him now would be like kicking her while she was down. My questions could wait. What was important was her.

Once she calmed down, I led her to a nearby coffee shop. We sat down at one of the small wooden tables and she let her backpack fall onto the floor.

"I can't believe this," she said as she rubbed her eyes. "He ran through a red light and a truck hit him. My car is totaled."

"I'm sorry," I said.

"And all he's worried about is himself. He's fine of course. Wouldn't surprise me if he was drinking, even this early. He wasn't on my insurance and even if they do pay something, it won't be enough for me to get a new car."

I tried to control my anger as I listened to her talk about Dennis.

"What kind of car would you get?" I asked. "If you could buy anything."

She laughed. "Yeah, we can play that game. Right now I'd be lucky if I can afford another piece of crap like the one I had."

"Don't think about that," I said. "Just get all that out of your mind and pretend. If money was no object, what kind of car would you buy?"

Jackie sighed and let out a small laugh as she shook her head. The waitress brought over two cups of coffee for us and Jackie warmed her hands around the mug.

"I know it sounds silly, but if I could have any car in the world it would be a Mini," she said.

I laughed. "A Mini? You could have any car in the world and you choose a Mini Cooper? Not a baby blue Maserati for example?"

"No," she said with a laugh. "That's not practical at all. I want something I don't have to worry about leaving in the grocery store parking lot."

"Alright, so practical. Two doors, four doors, what color?" I asked, mentally taking notes.

"Hmm, I think four doors so that when I get a dog he can easily hop into the back."

She really is perfect, I thought.

"I think I'd like it to be red with those cute white stripes," she said, relaxing. "And a sun roof."

"Sounds nice," I said.

She took a sip of her coffee then looked at me shyly.

"Thank you for being here," she said. "I know I don't deserve you hanging around and taking my mind off of things."

"Why do you say that?"

"Because I haven't been very nice to you at times," she said.

"Don't worry about it," I said as I took her hand. "I'll just add it to the running list of things you owe me for."

"You're terrible," she said with a laugh.

"Maybe, but you love it."

Chapter Eleven

Jackie

The doorbell woke me from a deep sleep. I heard Dennis grumbling as he opened the door. A few moments later, I heard him again.

"What the fuck," he said.

The door slammed and his feet stomped through the small apartment to my bedroom door. Hearing so much anger from him, I pulled the covers up to my chin for protection, despite wearing pajama pants and a tank top.

"Who the fuck have you been fucking?" he yelled as he threw open my door. "I knew you looked better lately. Did you find yourself one of those billionaires like your friends have? Wait until he finds out you're really a prude. Or maybe you just spread your legs for money."

I stared at him, taking all his jabs and insults. What made him talk to me like that? What was going on?

My first thought was to keep my mouth shut and just take it. I went with my second thought.

I jumped out of the bed and walked straight towards him.

"Get the fuck out," I yelled. "Who do you think you are for talking to me like that? I don't have to put up with this. You shouldn't even be here! You should've been gone last week."

He rolled his eyes like I was annoying him and turned his back to me. I didn't know what came over me, but my hands went up and shoved him as hard as I could.

Dennis stumbled out the bedroom door, tripping on the rug. When he caught his footing, he glared at me angrily then took a step towards me.

Was he going to hit me?

Without thinking, I took a step towards him and narrowed my eyes.

"Go ahead and try it," I said. "Watch what happens next."

He scowled as he stood his ground. I felt like he was waiting to see if I would turn away first, but I refused to. He looked away and then turned towards the door.

What happened? How did things get so bad, I wondered.

"You got a delivery," he said.

He opened the door and walked out.

I quickly grabbed my cardigan from the closet and put it on. In the doorway was an older man dressed in an outfit that reminded me of the bellhops at old hotels. He had on a long coat with matching pants and a hat with gold embroidery around the brim.

"Miss Jackie Stone?" he said.

"Yes?"

"I am Reginald Britton, butler for the Winslow family. Here are your keys." He held up a set of keys between his fingers.

"Keys?" I asked.

He jingled the keys in the air. Unsure what to do, I put my hand out and he dropped them into my palm. I held the plastic key fobs in my hand and marveled at how different they were from the metal car keys of my last car. Flipping a fob over, I recognized the Mini logo.

"There must be a mistake," I said holding them out to Reginald. "These aren't mine."

"I never make mistakes, miss. Your car is parked outside."

"Wait, what? My car?"

He started walking down the flight of stairs. I followed him to the parking lot across the street where a shiny, red, four-door Mini Cooper with white bonnet stripes was parked with a giant red bow on top. Even though the bow covered the roof, I knew there was a sun roof and everything else I daydreamed about to Brent.

I shrieked with excitement. I couldn't believe it belonged to me. But why? Why would he help me like that?

"Who's it from?" Dennis grunted as he flicked a cigarette butt to the ground.

"If I may, miss," Reginald said with his eyebrows raised.

I nodded, unsure what he was going to do.

"Sir, it is none of your business who it is from. It is a gift for Miss Stone. And if I hear you talk to her again the way you did earlier, you will be smoking those cigarettes out of your arse."

Giggling I opened the car door and breathed in the beautiful new car smell. I sat inside and took everything in. I couldn't believe it. I had never had a new car before, let alone one I dreamed up.

I removed the bow and carried it into my apartment, then quickly got dressed. Dennis was still outside, chain smoking. I didn't say anything to him as I walked past him. I got into the new car and drove to Winslow Environmental.

As I entered the glass building, the woman behind the reception desk stood and smiled at me like she knew me.

"Good morning, Miss Stone," she said. "Mr. Winslow is expecting you." The elevator doors dinged as they opened. "His office is on the twentieth floor."

Smiling at her, I got into the elevator and pinched myself as the doors closed. Everything was so surreal, I found it hard to believe I wasn't dreaming.

When the doors opened, a woman with a tightly wrapped bun and rust colored reading glasses was waiting for me.

"Good morning, Miss Stone," she said. "I'm Marcia, Mr. Winslow's personal assistant. If you have any problems with the car, if anything isn't precisely to your liking, please let me know."

I stared at her, unsure what to say.

"Thank you?" I said, hesitantly.

"Mr. Winslow is expecting you," she said. "Also, I took the liberty of ordering your favorite breakfast."

"Which is?" I asked, curious if she really knew.

"Brioche french toast and hash browns with warmed syrup and a glass of orange juice."

"Okay, this is too freaky," I said.

She laughed. "You'll get used to it."

"I don't think so," I said. "Where is he?"

"Right this way, miss."

I followed her down a long hall. At the end of the hall were open double doors. Marcia knocked on one of the doors and then waved me in. Brent was standing in front of the wide window looking at his view of Canyon Cove University. He smiled as he watched me enter the room.

"You got the gift?" he asked.

"Yes, thank you, but I can't accept it."

Marcia entered the office and placed my breakfast on a table with a white tablecloth, then left the room and closed the office doors.

"Are you going to tell me what this is all about?" I asked.

"I don't know what you're talking about," he said. "I do this for all my friends."

"Oh? What's Gunnar's favorite breakfast?"

"Black coffee with lots of sugar," he said.

"You're so full of shit." I shook my head.

I was flattered. Maybe I should have been nervous that he went out of his way to find out all these things about me, but it made me feel special. No one had ever made such a big deal about me before.

"You should eat your breakfast before it gets cold," he said.

"How did you know about this? Did Sam tell you?"

"I'll never reveal my secrets," he said with a grin.

"That Sam," I said shaking my head. "I'm worried what else she might have told you about."

"Don't worry, nothing embarrassing."

I started thinking about the things Samantha knew about me. She and I had been friends for so long, she was like the sister I never had. I thought about the things she might have told Brent and my exes came to mind.

"Did she tell you about Dennis?" I asked.

"Not really," he said as his mouth set in a fine line. "Only that you've been on and off for four years. In her defense, I asked her about him last night after he wrecked your car."

I nodded, understanding why he would be curious.

"What about Marc?" I asked.

"Who?" he asked, his brow furrowing.

"Nothing. Never mind."

My stomach growled hungrily. I sat down and Brent joined me at the table. While I ate, I thought about how he had been showing up wherever I was for months. I thought about the car he bought me, and I thought about breakfast. He wasn't treating me like someone he hated. Why did I ever think he felt that way about me?

As I finished eating, I pulled the Mini key fobs from my bag and set them in front of Brent.

"I can't take this," I said. "I love it, but it's too much. Take it back."

"If you don't want it, you can take it back and use the money for something else," he said. "It's your car, not mine. You needed a car and I got you one. Just enjoy it."

He slid an envelope across the table to me. I didn't have to open it to know it was the title.

"You're crazy," I said. "You're practically stalking me, you bought me a brand new car, and your evil proposition of having sex with me is all about my having multiple orgasms."

He laughed. "Tough life, huh?"

"I thought you hated me," I said.

He leaned back into his seat as he crossed his legs at the knee.

"Yes, you did think that, but I never knew why. I don't think I've ever acted like I hate you, have I?"

"No, you haven't," I said. "I guess I just thought that since I was such a bitch to you, that you should hate me."

"I don't think I could ever hate you."

"At least let me pay you for the car. Figure out a payment plan or something," I said.

"How about this," he said, leaning towards me. "How about you stop hating me? Just give me a chance and I'll say you paid for the car."

"That's ridiculous."

"So you can't stop hating me?" he asked.

"No, I can't. I stopped hating you a while ago."

Chapter Twelve

Jackie

I left Brent's office on cloud nine. I drove all around Canyon Cove from downtown, to South End, then onto the freeway and through the canyon road to the beach, before I headed home. I wanted to feel guilty for accepting such a huge gift, but Brent was so genuine about giving it to me that I only felt happy.

As I climbed the steps to the second floor of the apartment building, Dennis stood from where he was seated on the floor. He took a long drag off his cigarette and then tapped it out against the concrete wall.

I didn't say anything to him. I kept my eyes on the door and pretended he didn't exist.

"Jackie, come on," he said as I reached the door. "You know that's me. I'm sorry."

"Sorry?" I said. "Did you learn a new word?"

I put my key in the door and unlocked it, but I didn't enter. I knew he would follow me in.

"I'm trying to apologize to you," he said. "I saw that car and just lost it. I don't know why, maybe I was jealous, but I know I have no right to be."

"That's right, you don't."

"You've been nothing but nice to me," he said. "I know you have no reason to let me stay with you and yet every time I'm in a jam, I can always count on you to help me out."

I shrugged, trying to keep my anger, but listening to him made it slowly evaporate.

"It's what I do," I said.

"I know! That's what's so great about you. Whenever anyone needs help, you're right there to help them out. I remember that girl you worked with who was booted from her apartment. You found out at work that she was sleeping in her car and you let her stay on your couch for a couple of nights. You barely knew her."

"She was sleeping in the grocery store parking lot. I couldn't let her do that," I said.

"Or what about that woman with the seven kids that one year around Christmas. You barely earn enough to make ends meet, but you gave her money to buy a tree and presents for her children so they could have a Christmas."

I looked down at the floor. I hated talking about this stuff. I knew they were great things that I did, I knew people didn't usually help others, but I couldn't do that.

"You do all these things for people and never expect anything back," he said. "And after all that paying it forward, that billionaire buys you the car you've been drooling over for years," he said.

I shrugged and turned the doorknob, keeping my back to the door.

"I really don't want to talk about this," I said quietly.

"And that's another thing," he said. "You do all these things and never expect anything in return. I've probably taken advantage of that and I shouldn't have. You are a much better person than I will ever be."

I couldn't stand there listening to him go on and on about me. I didn't want to hear it. I pushed the door open and entered my apartment. Dennis came in behind me.

"I know you don't want me around," he said. "I know I cause more trouble than I'm worth and I'm not easy to deal with. I haven't said anything to you, but I'm going through a tough time right now. I got RIF'd last week."

"You were fired?"

"They downsized and I was one of the ones they let go with severance. I knew it was coming," he said. "I've been lucky you've been so nice about letting me stay here for so long, but I know I overstayed my welcome. If you could just give me a couple a days, I promise I'll be out of here and in a new place."

My lips twitched with all the words I kept to myself instead of saying to Dennis. Our relationship always had a lopsidedness that benefited him. He was egotistical, conniving, and didn't care about anyone but himself, but I never held that against him.

I made excuses for Dennis's behavior. I made excuses for most people. I believed Dennis was just how he was and there was no changing or fixing his behavior, that was just him.

The way I thought made it hard to stay angry at him. It was like being angry at a puppy who peed on the rug. It was pointless because the puppy didn't know any better. That's what I thought of Dennis. And that's why I always helped him.

I looked over at the couch and thought about my schedule for the next two days. I had to work both those nights and I needed to work on a paper for class. I probably wouldn't even be home anyway.

"Fine, you can stay," I said. "But only for two days. If you don't have an apartment after that, I can tell you about a nice parking spot at the grocery store. I'll even buy you a tent."

Chapter Thirteen

Brent

Weeks had gone by since I last saw Jackie. With the Thanksgiving holiday she was busy with classes and even more catering jobs.

I had backed off from showing up where she was to give her a break. Giving her the car was a little too much and with everything she was dealing with, I thought she needed a break. She was confused and I wondered if it had anything to do with her involvement with Dennis.

Reginald told me what he heard at her apartment when he dropped off the car. It took everything in me to not go over there and kick Dennis's ass. And if I was her boyfriend I would have done that, but I wasn't, he was.

The reason for his being at her apartment was clear to me. She must have loved him. In some weird, warped way, she had to love him. Why else would she put up with such an abusive person?

If Dennis was good to her, if he treated her well, then I would have backed away and let her be happy with him. But whether he was her boyfriend or not, he didn't treat her right. I knew I would.

It wasn't my place to judge her and her situation. I only wanted what was best for her. In time she would see that that was me.

I wanted to see her more. I wanted her to be mine. I wanted to show her what she was really worth. Instead, she was with him.

As I leaned back in my office chair, I thought about our arrangement. I hadn't pushed it any further because I knew I was falling for her. Each time I saw her, every time we were together, my feelings for her grew.

Originally I thought any time with her would be enough, but it wasn't. I wanted more. I had to make my move. She needed to know without any doubt how I felt about her. And I needed to know the same.

My private line rang. I tapped the speaker button as I put my feet up on the desk.

"Brent speaking," I said.

"Brent, it's Xander Boone. How have you been?"

"I'm good. I saw you've had some great acquisitions lately. Good to see the Boone name expanding again."

"We're growing slowly, but I'm moving into new markets. Some interesting technologies out there. If you're interested we should meet for a round of golf."

"No, that's more my brother's thing," I said. I got the invitation to your Christmas Eve party."

"That's great. Hopefully I'll see you there."

"You will," I said as an idea struck me. "Mind if I bring a date?"

"Of course not, the more the merrier."

"Great. Listen, Xander, I'll have to call you back. I have a few things I need to take care of. It was good hearing from you."

"I'll talk to you soon," Xander said as he hung up.

The Boone Christmas party was the perfect place to take Jackie on a date. It was someplace she'd be comfortable and familiar with everyone so we could focus on getting to know each other better.

I tapped the button for Marcia.

"Marcia, make reservations at the most romantic restaurant you can think of," I said.

"How about The Breezes? It's right on the ocean and has a beautiful view."

"That sounds perfect," I said.

"Do you want me to buy it out for the night?"

"No, just make sure we get a nice table away from everyone."

"Yes, sir. Anything else?"

"If I think of anything I'll let you know. Thank you."

I picked up Jackie's work schedule for the week. I was going to surprise her again. I wasn't going to let anything get in the way of being with her again.

Chapter Fourteen

Jackie

I set my tray down and pulled out my phone to see if I had any messages. *Why haven't I heard from Brent?* It had been two weeks since the day he gave me the car. What happened?

I kept playing things over and over in my head. I thought for sure that things would change between us, instead I didn't see him at all. I didn't realize how used to running into him I was until he wasn't around any more.

I missed him.

After loading my tray with champagne flutes I made my way around the wedding reception. It was a Saturday night, a big night for weddings at the Arc Hotel, even in the middle of December.

As the champagne disappeared from my tray, Jayne, one of the other waitresses, came over to me. She matched my pace as we walked through the room.

"Holy shit, you should see the wedding in the next room," she said.

"Fancy?" I asked.

"You wouldn't believe it. Apparently they had a beach wedding over the summer and already wanted to renew their vows."

"You've got to be kidding me," I said. "Seems like overkill."

"A waste of money if you ask me. When you get a chance you should check it out. They have photos from their first wedding outside their event room too. It's crazy."

"I think I'll pass," I said. "Nothing worse than a beach wedding anyway."

"Yeah, so cliché," Jayne said.

With my tray empty, I decided to disappear so I could send Brent a quick text. There was no reason why I couldn't text him. After all, he did say I knew how to reach him.

Jackie: Missing -- one stalker. Any idea where he went?

I waited for what felt like forever for Brent to finally respond.

Brent: I knew you'd miss me. I just handed over my car to the valet.
Jackie: Here?
Brent: Of course. You know how many weddings there are tonight? No best man can handle that amount of women, they'll need back up. You know I do my best work at weddings.
Jackie: You're such a jerk.
Brent: But you love me anyway.

I stared at the words on my screen. I knew he was just joking around as usual, but it hit home for me. He was right. After all that time of pushing him away, of trying to convince myself that I hated him, I was falling for him.

Jackie: Where are you?
Brent: I'm in the hall. I'll be there soon.

I couldn't wait to see him. As I stepped into the hall, I saw Brent at the other end. In between us was the other wedding with the photos on display at the entrance.

The loud music thumped as I walked towards Brent. One of the photos caught my attention out of the corner of my eye. I tried to ignore it, but something about it nagged at me.

As I turned to look at the photos, the bride and groom were in my direct line of sight as they cut the cake. The bride's wavy blonde hair bounced as she giggled, but it was the groom who caught my attention.

I couldn't take my eyes off him, but I could have looked away and still known what he looked like or how his dark brown hair fell over his left eye whenever he laughed. I would recognize the timbre of his voice or how his brow knitted when he looked at the cake. It was Marc.

My heart stopped and my mouth opened as I gasped for breath. I started to shake as I stood in the hall and watched as the couple smiled and laughed as they fed each other cake. Pain shot through my chest. As the room started to spin, I caught my first full look at the photos. They had a perfect summer day for their beach wedding at sunset.

I can't do this anymore. I just can't.

The tears started to fall before I realized I was crying, but they were welcome. I couldn't see the couple or their ridiculous oversized photos through the blur. Brent rushed over and put his arms around me.

"What happened, Jackie? Are you okay?" he asked, his voice filled with concern.

I turned towards him and tried to answer, but my throat tightened each time I attempted words. I nodded my head at him.

Yes, I'm okay, I'm alright. Just something huge flew into my eyes, I thought as I blinked and wiped at my tears.

But then Brent did the worst thing anyone could do. He hugged me. I couldn't keep it in anymore. I couldn't fight back the tears that had been waiting to break past the dam I built up. I clung to the lapels of Brent's jacket as all those years of stuffed down emotions flooded out of me. I was so consumed by my feelings I didn't realize I was spilling everything out for Brent to hear.

Five Years Ago

"Tomorrow's the big day," I said excitedly.

Marc and I walked down the hall side by side. As he walked, he responded to a text with a small smile. He laughed before typing more as his dark hair fell onto his forehead.

Everything was going to be perfect. We had just left the rehearsal dinner we put together for the twenty people coming to our wedding. I felt bad not being able to invite everyone we knew, but having a beach wedding on Avalon Island was so expensive we had to limit the invites.

When Marc and I first started planning the wedding, he told me about a perfect spot on Avalon Island. He said that was where we needed to get married and I agreed. It was a beautiful place. Originally, we wanted to get married as the sun set into the Pacific Ocean, but Marc changed his mind so we were going to have a morning wedding.

Avalon was just off the coast of Canyon Cove, but it was only accessible through boat or helicopter. We took the hour-long boat ride with our closest family and friends to get married and spend the weekend before Marc and I left for our honeymoon.

I waited patiently for Marc to say something. In the months before the wedding, he had become quieter, almost withdrawn. Whenever I asked him if there was something wrong, he said I was being overly sensitive and nothing was wrong with him. But he was on his phone more and sometimes when I went to bed early, I'd wake up and hear him talking in the other room. I didn't know who he was talking to, but I trusted him.

As we reached my room, Marc's brow furrowed as he looked at me.

"I'm sorry, did you say something?" he asked.

"It's okay, it was nothing important," I said as I unlocked the door.

"Okay, well I'll see you tomorrow."

"The big day," I said grinning.

"Yup, the big day." He said matter-of-factly. "You know I think this separate room thing is ridiculous."

"It's just for one night."

"We sleep together every night. We own a house together. Why can't we stay together tonight?"

"It's bad luck for the groom to see the bride before the wedding."

"Give me a break," he said. "You don't really believe that, do you? What could possibly happen?"

I shrugged. "Struck by lightning? Or maybe you'll change your mind."

He tilted his head to the side and smiled.

"We're getting married tomorrow, why would I change my mind about that?" he said.

His phone buzzed in his pocket, but he ignored it.

"Then you can wait just one more night," I said as I shooed him away from the door. "We've been together for five years, and tomorrow is the first day of the rest of our lives together."

He groaned and rolled his eyes.

"I knew you'd love that," I said with a laugh.

"Fine," he said with a sigh. "I'll sleep all by myself in my little hotel room while you enjoy this suite." He looked into the room. "That looks much more comfortable than mine."

"You'll be here tomorrow night," I said.

His phone buzzed again and he looked at his watch.

"It's almost midnight," he said. "I guess I should get out of here before you turn into a pumpkin or lose your shoe or something."

I nodded. "Yes, go."

With a playful push, he left the room.

***

Where is he?

I peeked out the sheer curtains. Through the window I could make out the sand-covered platform we would stand on to take our vows. Everyone was casually dressed, just as we requested. I didn't see the point in them getting all dressed up for a casual beach wedding. It was something Marc and I disagreed about, but he caved in. The only thing we asked was that they wouldn't wear something blue.

On a trip to Puerto Rico several months ago, Marc found a pale blue guayabera shirt with embroidered palm trees. I wasn't crazy about it, but he loved it and wanted to wear it for the wedding. I thought he could be my something blue and agreed to it.

Samantha came up behind me and gingerly put her hand on my shoulder. The warmth of her hand on my dress's lace sleeve comforted me but worried me at the same time. Even though I knew the answer, I still had to ask.

"Have you heard anything?" I asked.

Samantha was pretty in a pale yellow dress that made her hair look coppery. As I searched her eyes for an answer, a pained look flashed across her face before she shook her head.

"He's probably just running late," she said.

I shook my head at Sam. "The wedding was supposed to start an hour ago. Marc is never late."

A knock at the door made us turn around. I hurried over and swung the door open hoping to see Marc. Instead it was his best friend, Paul.

"Anything?" I blurted out as he entered the room.

Paul's brows knitted together as his mouth hung open just a little.

"Just say it," I said. "Just spit it out."

"He's still not answering his phone. I went to the front desk and they said he checked out early this morning and left on the 5am boat back to the mainland," he said.

"What? Why? Did something happen? Was there an emergency?" I asked. "His family is here, his friends are here, why would he leave?"

"I...I don't know," he stammered, unable to look me in the eye. "But they gave me this."

Paul handed me a small envelope with my name on it. I opened it and unfolded the ivory hotel stationary. I recognized Marc's handwriting immediately.

Jackie,
I can't do this. Don't hate me. I'm sorry.
Love,
Marc

I stared at the words on the paper and read them over again. No matter how many times I read them, they didn't make sense.

"I have to get home," I said. "He must have gone home."

"I'll go outside and tell everyone," Samantha said softly.

I blinked at her as I made sense of her words. Nothing was connecting for me. I didn't understand what happened, but I must have done something. Maybe I should have let him stay the night in the suite. Maybe we'd be married by now.

"No, they came here for us, for our wedding. I should tell them."

"Are you sure?" Paul asked. "They'll understand if it comes from someone else."

"No, I should do this," I said.

As I left the room, Samantha caught up to me.

"Are you okay?" she asked.

"I'm fine," I said.

I wasn't. Inside, my heart felt like it was trapped in a vise grip, but I didn't have time to think about how awful I felt. I had to get back home.

I didn't know what happened, but the quicker I could leave that island the better. Marc had to be at home. I would find him and we'd talk about this. We had been together for five years, and if he wasn't ready to get married, that was fine. I could wait.

***

Everything that happened after reading Marc's note was a blur. I told everyone that Marc rushed home for an emergency. It was the only thing that made sense to me. I couldn't tell them that the wedding was off. They were smart enough to figure that out themselves.

I turned away from the pity in their eyes. I shrugged away from the embraces of comfort. I could keep it together if no one touched me so I avoided them all. I left as quickly as I could to pack and caught the next boat back.

Samantha wanted to come with me, but I told her I needed to see Marc by myself. On the boat, I sat alone on a bench and watched the seagulls as they stole food from unsuspecting passengers. I checked my phone for any new messages and tried Marc's number again. Nothing.

My mind raced.

Is he sick?
Did the kennel call?
Did our house catch fire?
Did he stop loving me??

I shoved that last one all the way in the back of a dark closet in my mind. I didn't want to think about it. I couldn't. I needed to keep it together and give him the benefit of the doubt. He said he loved me. He didn't want to sleep without me last night. That had to count for something.

As soon as the boat docked, I jumped into the nearest taxi and gave the driver our address. I didn't see Marc's car in the driveway, but that didn't mean anything.

Maybe he went to pick up the dog.
Maybe he went to pick me up at the dock.
Maybe he's gone.

I shoved that thought away as I fumbled with the lock on the front door. It finally clicked and pushed the door open, hoping to find Marc smiling at me like he did whenever I came home.

The house was empty. The furniture was gone. My stomach dropped and churned and I couldn't catch my breath. I thought I was going to be sick, but I shoved that into the closet with the other thoughts and feelings I didn't want to deal with.

I raced through the house. Everything was gone except for our bedroom. The bed was made and everything in that one room looked just like I left it. It made the emptiness of the house that much worse.

As my chest began to ache I looked at the dresser. I knew what wasn't in the drawers. I knew what was missing from the closet. I didn't have to look. I knew Marc was gone.

My mind went blank. I tried to figure out what happened, where he went, why he would do something like this.

If he was unhappy why didn't he just talk to me?

But I didn't want to deal with the thoughts spinning in my mind. I swallowed hard as I pushed back everything into that closet that was getting too crowded in the back of my head and pulled my shoulders back.

I don't need him.

I don't need anyone.

I can take care of myself.

Footsteps echoed in the foyer and I rushed out of the bedroom.

"Marc?" I called out.

"No, dear, it's me," said Mrs. Lean, our neighbor. "This old house looks so much bigger when it's empty. Did you sell it? I didn't even know you were moving."

"Neither did I," I said.

"Oh dear. And isn't today..." Her forehead wrinkled and she tilted her head away from me.

She feels bad for me. That's the same look everyone had at the wedding.

She hugged herself, wrapping her thick arms around her floral housecoat as she looked around the empty room.

"You don't have to stay," I said. "It's okay."

"I saw him this morning with that friend of yours," she said.

"Friend?" I asked, confused.

"Oh dear," she muttered, "I knew she wasn't your friend." She clicked her tongue against the roof of her mouth. "Pretty thing with wavy blonde hair, sound familiar?"

She waited for me to answer and as I closed my eyes, I sighed and nodded yes.

"Marc got a new assistant a few months ago," I said. "Ginny. She giggled every time I called.

I thought she was just a ditz, but I guess she was just laughing at how stupid I am."

"You're not stupid, dear. You were in love. Although love does make us stupid," she said with a gentle smile. "They would come here for lunch. I ran into them once or twice and he told me she was your friend. I wanted to say something to you, but I kept telling myself it was none of my business. I'm sorry."

I thought about how many times I had asked Marc to meet me during lunch so we could finalize our wedding plans, but he was always busy. Ginny.

Fucking Ginny.

"Wait a second," I said. "I know where she lives."

I ran to the garage and lifted the door. Mrs. Lean followed me, looking excited.

"What are you going to do?" she asked.

"I don't know. But he can't just leave like this. And on our wedding day too. I'm going to give them both a piece of my mind. He can't treat me like this."

"Go get him," she said as she pumped her wrinkled fist in the air.

I drove frantically to her apartment on the other side of town. I ran through stop signs, I made illegal turns, I didn't care. I needed to get there as quickly as I could.

Was he moving in?
Where they getting a place together?
Were they going to get married?

I opened my mind's closet door and tossed that last one in before quickly closing it. I didn't need any of those things to start tumbling out now.

As I pulled up I thought of all the great things I would say to Marc. I thought about how I wasn't going to cry. I was going to show him that he couldn't break me, he couldn't destroy me. I was going to be just fine without him.

A U-Haul was parked in front of her apartment. As she carried out a lamp, Marc appeared from inside the truck, took the lamp, and gave her a kiss.

It wasn't a sweep-her-off-her-feet kind of kiss, just a sweet peck on the lips. But it stopped me dead in my tracks. I stood frozen to the sidewalk, maybe a hundred feet from them, but they didn't see me. They were in their own little world.

I didn't know how long I stood there, but each time she handed him something, he did something sweet. A kiss. A smile. A lingering touch of his hand.

He's in love with her.

These were all the little things I wished for from him. Things I had spoken to him about, but was told he wasn't that kind of guy. He didn't think of it, it wasn't part of him, he would never be that cuddly, physical man.

But he is for her.

As he closed up the U-Haul and gave Ginny a big hug, I realized he was wearing the blue shirt he bought for our wedding.

My chest ached. It felt like Marc had reached inside and was squeezing everything out of my heart. I hugged myself as I realized tears had been rolling down my cheeks.

No! Not now.

I didn't want to deal with this. I didn't want these emotions. I refused to cry and feel sorry for myself.

I am strong.
I am independent.
I am broken.

I shoved that last one under the closet door in my mind. I would never allow anyone to see that.

Present Day

I wiped my eyes as I finally calmed down, woozy and out of breath. My chest still ached, but I knew I was going to be alright. Brent led me down the hall to a small alcove with a couch.

He kept his arm around my shoulders as we sat down, holding me close. He must have had a ton of questions, but he didn't say or ask me anything and I was grateful for that.

I didn't know if I could talk about it yet. I had spent so long hiding my feelings about it, stuffing them away into the darkest corner in my mind, trying to be strong, that I didn't realize how much Marc had really hurt me.

As I breathed in deep, I thought about Marc smiling happily with his bride. I wanted to hate her. I wanted to think of her as a bitch for breaking us up, but I knew it wasn't her fault. Our relationship had problems and for Marc she was the solution.

Fucking Ginny.

He loved her so much that they renewed their vows within a year of their marriage. I couldn't even get him to show up to our wedding.

I held onto all of that for so long, I thought it was part of me. I thought I was destined to never be happy. I believed I'd have to keep stuffing down my feelings because no one would ever care.

It took seeing Marc married for me to realize what happened wasn't my fault. Maybe it wasn't even his fault. Despite what I wanted to believe for all these years, Marc and I didn't work as a couple. There was never any passion there.

All my tears opened my eyes to the pain I kept inside all those years. Shutting it away didn't do anything but hold me in the past. Now that I let it out I felt ready to move forward. I was ready to think about a life that wasn't tainted by my memories of Marc.

Leaning forward, I rested my elbows on my knees and covered my face with my hands. I didn't want him seeing me with my red face and puffy eyes. Brent's hand gently stroked my back. I peeked at him from the corner of my eye and he smoothed my escaping hair back behind my ear.

I thought about all the time I spent hating him, but that was a lie. It had nothing to do with Brent or anything he did, it was me. I hated that Brent made me feel vulnerable. I hated that I loved spending time with him. I hated that by his being nothing like Marc or Dennis, he reminded me of how bad my past relationships really were and how much I deserved better. But mostly, I hated that I was falling in love with him.

Brent had become the one man in my life who I could count on. He never made me feel bad. If anything he always seemed to know how to make me feel better. And whether it was fate or his uncanny timing, he was always there whenever I needed someone the most.

"Why are you here?" I asked. "Why are you always here? Whenever I've needed someone lately, somehow you just show up."

"Because from the first moment I saw you, I knew you needed someone. I want to be that someone," he said.

"You just want sex," I said, forcing a laugh.

"Stop it, Jackie." He knelt down in front of me so I had no choice but to look at him. "I've been doing whatever I can to be with you. You have no idea how much I hate these events, but I will go to one every night of the week if it means I get to spend a few minutes with you."

I shook my head and hid my face in my hands again.

"You're crazy," I said.

"Crazy for you."

"And you're cheesy too."

He laughed as he pulled my hands away from my face.

"I'm tired of this, Jackie. I'm tired of playing games to get more time with you. Let me take you out to dinner."

"As in a date?" I asked.

"Yes, a date, next Saturday."

"Next Saturday? You've been stalking me for months and now you want to wait over a week?"

He grinned and laughed softly.

"I have to go away next week. There's an environmental conference I'm attending in Geneva. Why don't you come with me?"

"To Geneva?"

It took me by surprise, but I couldn't imagine wanting to do anything more. I could get away from the ghost of Marc, from the ever-present Dennis, and maybe start on my future with Brent. But just as I was going to say yes, I remembered I had booked myself solid with work. Not only that, but I had finals that week.

"I wish I could go, but I can't. With work and finals, I can't do it," I said.

Disappointment flashed across his face.

"Then promise you'll join me for dinner when I get back," he said. "Then after dinner I want to show you off as my date at the Boone Christmas party. What do you say?"

I didn't need to think about it. My head was nodding before the word came out of my mouth.

"Yes."

Chapter Fifteen

Jackie

As I stared into my closet I realized I had nothing to wear for my date with Brent. Sure, the closet was packed tight and there were things in there that hadn't seen the light of day in a long time, but tonight was a big deal. Tonight I was going on my first date in years.

I grabbed my bag and headed straight for the door. It was just past noon so I had enough time to get to the mall for an hour and then get back and get ready.

"Where are you going?" Dennis asked as he looked up from a magazine.

I sighed as I stopped in the doorway. Why didn't I kick him out? Why was I always being so nice to him? He didn't deserve it at all.

"I'm going to the mall," I said. "I have a date tonight so I'd appreciate it if you disappeared."

He set the magazine down on the coffee table.

"Mind if I tag along?" he asked. "I won't get in your way, I just need to pick up a new pair of jeans."

"Fine," I said, not wanting any more delays. "Just hurry up. I don't have a lot of time."

"Okay, okay," he said, holding up his hands as if he was at gunpoint.

He got up and grabbed his wallet off the table as I stepped out the door.

Dennis snorted softly as we reached my new car. Out of the corner of my eye I saw his face squish into a pained look.

"You don't have to come with me, you know," I said.

"No, no, I really need a new pair of jeans."

"You made a face," I said.

"I had something caught in my throat," he said.

He made a similar sound to his snort several times as he cleared his throat.

"Asshole," I said under my breath as I unlocked the car.

We drove in silence to the mall. There was more traffic on the roads than I expected so I kept looking at the clock and ticking down in my head how much time I had before I needed to get back home.

I wished I was alone. I regretted having him tag along, but I didn't want to hear him complain about my leaving him behind. I was also hopeful that if I was nice to him, he would be nice back by going out tonight.

"I was thinking that maybe you should buy an air bed or something. Your couch isn't very comfortable," he said.

"It's not meant to be slept on," I said. "Shouldn't your apartment be ready by now?"

"I've been meaning to talk to you about that," he said. "You know they were painting my place, well they decided to renovate the whole building and then sell it. I need to find a new place to live."

"So then find one," I said as I pulled into the mall's parking garage.

I was tired of all his excuses. He needed to get out of my apartment.

"I was thinking maybe I should buy something. We make a good team and--"

"Don't even finish that thought. I don't want to hear it," I said.

I parked the car and hurried towards the entrance. Dennis rushed to catch up with me, but I wasn't in the mood. I was there for one purpose--to find the cutest thing possible to wear tonight.

"Let me finish," he said. "We could buy a place together and the mortgage will save us money instead of us paying rent separately."

"Have you lost your mind? I don't want to buy a house with you. I don't want to live with you either. I only let you stay with me because you don't have anywhere else to go."

Even as I said it, I began to question it. Dennis always had a lot of friends. And even though he hadn't said anything about his dating, I knew it wasn't like him to be alone for as long as he had been.

He followed me through the department store and into the mall.

"Why are you following me? I thought you needed to get jeans," I said.

He winced and raised his eyebrows at me. I hated acting like a bitch, but Dennis deserved it.

Oh no, now he's going to make me feel guilty. Don't do it, Jackie. Don't do it!

"There's a new style I want to try on," he said. "I need your opinion on how they look."

"Are you kidding me?"

"I promise it won't take long," he said, his eyes pleading with me.

Don't do it!

"Just one pair?" I asked.

"Just one. I swear," he said. "I know you don't have a lot of time."

Sighing, I looked at the stores surrounding us. Dennis's favorite store was on the way to Torque, my favorite clothing store. Despite how much I wanted to, I couldn't say no. I was too nice. Sometimes I hated myself for that.

"Alright, fine," I said. "But just one pair."

We entered the store and Dennis went straight for the wall with its shelves of jeans. I wandered over to a circular rack with shirts hanging on it and checked the time.

Forty-five minutes.

Dennis took a small stack of jeans into the dressing room. A minute later he stepped out in one of the jeans and walked to the three way mirror.

"What do you think?" he asked.

I glanced at his jeans.

"They look fine," I said.

"It looks like I don't have an ass. They look baggy back there."

"Are you serious?"

"See?" he asks.

He tugs the seat of the jeans and I nod. He was right, the jeans were baggy.

"Gimme a sec to try on another pair," he said.

Before I could answer he disappeared into the dressing room again. After a minute he stepped out in a pair of really faded jeans.

"These look like something out of the eighties," he said. "I have another pair to try."

Sighing, I looked at my watch again as he changed. *How did ten minutes pass?*

"Dennis," I said as I knocked on his door, "We have to leave in half an hour. I'm going to the store."

He opened the door and stepped out in another pair of jeans that fit perfectly.

"No, wait," he said. "I think these are it, but the denim is kinda thin." He waved over a petite blonde with french braids who was behind the cash register. "Do you have this fit in another style?"

She looked at the tags and nodded. "We do. They should be on the wall."

"I grabbed all the jeans in my size," he said.

"Let me check in the back," she said. "If anyone asks, tell them Molly is helping you."

As she walked away, Dennis started roaming the store. I was beginning to really lose my patience. I looked at the time and shook my leg nervously as Dennis wandered.

"I'm going to get going," I said.

"This will only be a minute," he said. "Just be patient."

"No, I'm running out of time. I need something for tonight. I came here for me, not you."

"Selfish much?" He turned around and started to look at some other clothing. "They have a women's section here. Why don't you look while I'm waiting on my jeans?"

"You know this store doesn't fit me right," I said. "It's like they think women should be built without any curves at all. Plus this place just isn't me."

I looked around the store to see if Molly was looking for us, but I didn't see her.

Where'd she go?

I didn't know why I stayed in that store. I should have left and gone shopping on my own, but I didn't. I hated that Dennis knew me so well that he knew I wouldn't leave.

When Molly came back she threw her hands up and shook her head.

"We're all out. Do you want me to check another store?" she asked as she returned to the register.

"That would be great," Dennis said with a smile.

I joined him at the register and tapped my foot impatiently.

Twenty minutes.

I still had enough time to find something, just not as much time as I wanted.

"Oh they have your size at Fashion Plaza," she said. "Do you want me to put them on hold for you?"

"That's only ten minutes from here," Dennis said. "We can make it."

"No we can't," I said. "You can go back out if you want to."

"On Christmas Eve? By myself?"

He tilted his head to the side like he always did when he wanted me to feel bad, but it didn't work this time.

"I have a date tonight," I said, trying to not shriek. "I came here to buy myself something new. I didn't come here to get you new jeans."

"Umm excuse me," Molly said. "I couldn't help but overhear. I don't know which store you were going to, but some of the stores are closing early tonight."

My eyes widened as her words sunk in. I knew my luck and thinking about Torque being closed made me want to wring Dennis's neck even more.

Without a word, I left the store and continued down towards Torque. I only had ten minutes, but it was enough time to find a few things and buy them. I'd figure everything else out at home.

As I approached the store, I could already see the large glass doors being pulled shut. I stopped and just stared at the store, seeing a few things on the mannequins that would have been perfect.

Fuck! Just my luck.

Dennis stood beside me.

"Oh hey, that sucks," he said. "I'm sorry."

After glaring at him I started to walk back towards the parking garage. I was in such a bad mood I just wanted to get out of the mall and get back home. I didn't have time to race around the mall trying to find open stores for a new outfit.

As I merged onto the freeway, my stomach dropped. Every lane was backed up. Traffic wasn't going anywhere.

"Guess there was an accident," Dennis said.

I'm never making it home on time now.

***

Stuck in traffic, I kept looking at the time as I silently counted down when Brent would pick me up for dinner. I wanted to call him and let him know I was running late, but with Dennis sitting next to me I couldn't. I didn't want him hearing me on the phone while I spoke to Brent. I'd have to wait until I got home.

I got home with fifteen minutes to spare. I ran into the apartment and took the quickest shower of my life. As much as I didn't want Dennis there in the beginning, I was a little glad he was there now. He could answer the door when Brent came while I finished getting ready.

As I swept the blush brush onto the apples of my cheeks, I checked my phone. Brent was ten minutes late. I was disappointed but relieved at the same time. If he was late, that meant I wasn't.

Finally looking at myself in the mirror, I thought I looked pretty good. All that rushing had helped give my skin a nice glow and for whatever reason, my hair was looking really good.

I left my bedroom and found Dennis sitting on the couch, flipping through the channels. He reeked of smoke.

"Were you outside?" I asked.

He groaned. "I told you I don't smoke in here."

"No, thats not what I meant. You don't need to be so defensive."

"You bring it out in me," he said.

Please just stop, I thought.

"I don't want to fight," I said. "I was just curious if you went for a walk or something."

He glanced over at me and then back at the television.

"You didn't miss him," he said. "He hasn't shown up."

Ouch.

"Oh," I said. "Okay, thanks."

"You'd might as well sit down," he said. "You might be waiting a while."

"What's that supposed to mean?" I asked, trying to keep the anger out of my voice.

"Nothing," he said with a shrug.

I sat on the couch and waited for Brent to come. I watched as the time ticked by painfully slowly. Why it couldn't move this slow when I was shopping, I didn't know. Now I wished it would speed up so Brent and I could go out.

I checked my phone for any new texts and any calls I didn't see come through, but nothing came. Once he was thirty minutes late, I checked the traffic to see if it was still bad, but it had cleared. There was no reason for Brent to not be there.

My brain spun as I thought of excuses for him.

He had an accident.
There's a family emergency.
He got a flat tire.
He's standing me up.

I hugged myself as I thought about the last one. I wanted to shove it away in the dark closet in the back of my head, but I couldn't.

The remembered pain of what I went through with Marc was still too close to the surface. But this felt even worse.

Brent knows what I went through with that. How could he do this to me? Why?

I grabbed my favorite sweater from the closet and stepped outside. The cool air snapped me out of the moment. He had to have a reason.

As I pulled open his contact information, my finger hovered over his name. I was going to call him and find out what happened. I wasn't going to let him treat me like this.

But I couldn't do it. I couldn't call him. I was afraid of what he would say. In the back of my mind I thought about how he used to hate me. How he hated me so much that he brought a date to Samantha's dinner. He had to know she was setting us up.

Maybe he still hated me. Maybe he was so cruel that he wanted to really hurt me. But why?

When I thought of our time together the past couple of months, none of it made any sense to me.

The door to my apartment opened and Dennis leaned against the doorway.

"Let's go get a drink," he said.

It was Christmas Eve and Brent wasn't coming. The last thing I wanted was to sit at home thinking about that.

***

Dennis drove to a new bar in downtown Canyon Cove. We entered a large open room with tables, chairs, and intimate booths in the corners. Every seat was taken. I thought people would be home with their families, but the bar was surprisingly crowded. A couple rose from their table as we walked past.

"We're heading out," the woman said as she touched my sleeve. "You can sit here."

"Thanks," I said.

As I squeezed between the tables to get to the empty seat, Dennis sat down on a wood chair. He surveyed the room and then his hand went up. A pretty waitress with braces on her teeth smiled as she walked over with a small drink tray.

"I'll have a vodka cranberry," he said, then pointed to me. "And she'll have a margarita on the rocks, no salt."

I nodded. I didn't drink much, but when I did margaritas were my favorite.

Hoping to hear something from Brent, I pulled my phone out to check it again. *Still nothing.*

"He's not going to call," Dennis said.

"How would you know?" I asked.

"Because I wouldn't," he said. "I guess he got what he wanted from you. Be glad, not many women get a car in exchange."

"And that right there is why we're never getting back together," I said.

"You're going to bring this up now?"

"Why do you always have to do that? Why do you always have to take the knife and twist it? Like I'm not feeling bad enough?"

"Oh here we go again," he said. "You're always reading into everything I say."

"I am? Then how else should I take that?" I asked.

The waitress put our drinks down and disappeared. I stirred my drink, stabbing at the ice cubes, while I waited for Dennis's response.

"Well?" I asked.

"Jeez, calm down. Just forget I said anything."

I was about to tear into him more when a man in a black suit with blond hair caught my eye. Brent was standing at the bar talking to his friend Gunnar Craven. I really did have the worst luck.

Of all the places Dennis could've taken me, he takes me to the same one Brent is at.

"Guess I can cross off accident and family emergency," I said.

"What?" Dennis said. "I didn't hear you."

"Nothing, forget about it," I said, unable to stop staring at Brent.

Dennis followed my gaze.

"Is that him?" he asked. "Do you want to go somewhere else?"

"I'm fine."

I said the words more to myself than to Dennis. Despite how upset I was, despite how much my blood sped up in my veins and despite my nervous habit of wringing my hands being on full display, I knew I would be alright. I didn't need to run away.

***

Dennis kept the drinks coming. I was deep into my third margarita, still watching Brent, when my margarita induced courage reared its head.

"I'm going over there," I said, slurring my words. "I'm going to give that asshole a piece of my pie. I mean mind. A piece of my mind."

Dennis laughed. "Now, now, Jackie. You know that's just the tequila talking. Maybe I should get you home."

"Who does he think he is? After all this time, after stalking me like some crazy person, who thinks he does? I mean who does he think he is?"

Dennis waved to the waitress and made a motion in the air like he was signing something. It caught me completely off guard and suddenly I thought it was the funniest thing I had ever seen.

I started laughing. First they were small giggles, but the more I thought about Dennis signing the air, the funnier it seemed to me.

"You're drunk," he said. "As soon as I get the bill, we're leaving."

"No! No no no," I said. "He's right there. I have to say something to him. Oh maybe I'll throw a drink in his face. I always wanted to do that."

"No, I'm not going to let you do that. You'll regret that in the morning. I'm taking you home before you embarrass yourself."

"Fine," I said.

I looked at my phone again. It was on and it looked like it was working, but I had my doubts. Maybe the line was messed up. Maybe he tried calling and it didn't go through.

With my margarita courage, I tapped Brent's contact information. I looked up at him at the bar again, then back at his number. I wasn't drunk enough to call him, but I was drunk enough to text him.

Jackie: Thanks for tonight, asshole.

Staring at the sarcastic words on the screen was sobering. I didn't press send. I didn't see the point in it.

Dennis reached across the table and roughly grabbed my arm then pulled me past the table. My phone fumbled in my hands until it dropped to the floor. As I picked it up, the phone buzzed letting me know the message was sent.

Crap! Oh well, it could have been worse.

Dennis put his hand on my back and led me out of the bar and into the crisp night air.

I tossed my phone into my bag and buried it underneath my wallet. I wasn't going to check it again for the rest of the night. Out of sight, out of mind.

Before I knew it I was back home and crawling fully dressed into my bed. For a brief moment I felt bad about Dennis sleeping on the couch, but it quickly left my mind. I hoped the whole day would too.

Chapter Sixteen

Brent

The airplane jerked as it touched ground at Canyon Cove Airport. I never liked flying on a holiday and flying on Christmas Eve reminded me why. Gunnar and I switched our phones off airplane mode and checked for any new email. My phone blinked as it registered a voicemail from Sam.

"Are you seeing your family tonight?" Gunnar asked.

"No, not until tomorrow," I said. "I actually have a date tonight."

"On Christmas Eve?"

"I've waited long enough. I even invited her to go to Geneva for the conference."

"What? And ruin our bromantic time together?" he asked, grinning.

"Gimme a break. When we weren't at the conference you were out fucking anything in a skirt."

"What can I say? I like skirts. You need to loosen up more."

"I'm loose enough already," I said. "Are you heading back to New York?"

"I'll be around for the next couple of days. An old friend of mine opened a new bar downtown last week and I did a little viral thing for him to get the business going. I'm hanging around to make sure everything goes well for him. If you and Jackie are downtown, stop on by."

After we got off the plane, Gunnar ran into a flight attendant he met up with regularly. I didn't wait for an introduction, I couldn't keep up with Gunnar's many female friends. I left him and got into the black Town Car that was waiting for me. As the car exited the airport, I called Sam back.

"Hey," she said, answering the phone. "I've been worried about you. Drake said you'd be back yesterday."

"Is everything alright?" I asked. "Did something happen to Shade?"

"He's fine. He's been sleeping in the baby's room every night. I don't think he's going to want to go home with you," she said with a laugh. "I was just worried because you didn't call."

"Sorry, it was the trip from Hell," I said. "Flights leaving Geneva were delayed because of a storm, then we missed our connecting flight. They need more connecting flights to Canyon Cove."

"Why didn't you charter a private jet?" she asked.

"You know how I feel about that," I said.

"Yes, I know. Right about now is when Drake would call you a do-gooder."

I laughed. "Hey, do you think you could do me a favor? Can Shade stay with you for just one more night?"

I looked at the time and realized I needed to head straight to Jackie's to pick her up for our date.

"Sure, that's no problem," she said. "But why? You usually pick him up right away."

"I have some things I need to do before the Boone Christmas party," I said, hoping she wouldn't probe any further.

I didn't want to tell Sam about my date with Jackie and since she didn't mention it, I assumed Jackie hadn't told her either. We had enough pressure from her the past couple of months, we didn't need it on our date.

"Oh? You're going? I didn't think that was your kind of thing," she said.

I muted the phone and gave the driver Jackie's address, then went back to the call.

"I don't know, I thought it would be nice. Xander and I know most of the same people, plus you and Drake will be there, right?"

"Of course. I wouldn't miss it."

"I'll see you later then," I said.

Several minutes later the driver turned off the freeway. Jackie's building was at the end of a block with a mixture of stores and apartments. It was a nice area just outside downtown Canyon Cove that had seen a lot of growth in the past couple of years.

The Mini I bought Jackie was parked on the street, not far from where I found her cursing her old car just a couple months ago. I grinned as I thought about her cursing at her old car to start. Running into her that day was no accident, but it was one of the little things I couldn't tell her about. It was better that she thought that every time we ran into each other was a coincidence, not something I planned.

As I walked up the cement steps to the second floor, I caught the smell of a cigarette burning. Leaning against Jackie's door was a man with messy hair and a bright orange and yellow striped shirt. I didn't need anyone to tell me this was Dennis.

I didn't know what to think about seeing him there. I couldn't forget what he told me on the phone after the wedding, but it didn't sound like the Jackie I knew. My instincts said she was mine, but what if I was wrong?

Dennis blew a long stream of smoke out, then tossed the cigarette onto the floor as he watched me approach. I wanted to punch him, and after what Reg told me I probably should have. But I knew Jackie wouldn't approve.

"Oh hey," he said, his mouth twitching. "Brent, right?"

"Is she inside?" I asked, reaching for the doorknob.

"No, she went out."

"Out?" I asked, raising an eyebrow.

I pushed the door open and caught a glimpse of her small apartment before he slammed the door shut.

"Yes, out," he said. "I told you she likes to fuck with men. You didn't really think she was going on a date with you, did you? She told me she didn't want to see you anymore."

I stared at Dennis and felt my fists clench as I gritted my teeth.

I was done. Whatever the truth was didn't matter. What I knew for sure was that Dennis was living there. Dennis was answering her phone. Dennis treated her like shit and she allowed it. It wasn't my fight to win for her. Things were too complicated.

"You win," I said.

I turned around and walked back down the steps to the waiting car. It was too much. Was she with him? Wasn't she? None of it mattered anymore.

***

I didn't know how long I had been at the bar with Gunnar and I didn't care. Gunnar's flight attendant friend was sitting at a table with several other women. Despite our friendship, I was surprised he wasn't spending his time with them.

"Come on, Brent, let's just sit down," Gunnar said. "You can't stand here all night."

"I don't want to sit," I said. "You don't need to babysit me, you can join your friends."

"No, they're not friends like you. You know the bro code, you never leave a man while he's down," he said. "I'm still surprised you didn't punch that fucker though."

I shrugged. "There was no point in it. She wasn't home. Whether he was telling the truth about her or not, he didn't lie about that."

"Maybe she forgot. We were away for a week. Why didn't you call her?"

"She told me she'd either be working or studying for finals," I said. "Add in the time zone difference and I didn't want to bother her."

"I've said it once and I'll say it again. You're a pussy."

"I'm not in the mood," I said. "Can't you be serious for once?"

"This from the man who used to always say life was too short to be serious."

I sighed, annoyed at Gunnar and pissed off at myself. My cell phone buzzed in my pocket. I looked at it and saw a text.

Jackie: Thanks for tonight, asshole.

Yup, asshole. She got that right, I thought.

As I put my phone away, something familiar caught my eye. I turned around to see what it was and recognized the orange and yellow striped shirt from earlier.

Dennis, that fucking dick.

He was walking through the main room of the bar with his hand on the small of Jackie's back.

I elbowed Gunnar and he turned around.

"Guess there's my answer right there," I said. "He's her boyfriend."

Chapter Seventeen

Jackie

I twisted my hair around and then flipped it through an elastic band as I left my bedroom. The bathroom door was open while Dennis looked at himself in the mirror. I grabbed the blanket hanging over the back of the couch as I turned on the TV with the remote control and dropped onto the couch.

"What are you doing?" Dennis asked. "Aren't you coming with me?"

"Out with your friends on New Year's Eve? No, that's just weird. I'll feel out of place."

"What are you talking about? You know everyone and they love you. You can't spend New Year's Eve by yourself."

"I'm not," I said. "There will be Ryan Seacrest and millions of people watching with me."

"Get dressed, Jackie," he said. "Either I'm staying here or you're coming with me."

"You know that's not fair," I said as I got up and turned off the TV. "You know I'd never be able to handle the guilt if you stayed home."

"I know, now hurry up. You know I hate being late."

***

We joined Dennis's friends at a new restaurant in the South End of Canyon Cove. As we entered I spotted Becca rubbing her arms as she looked around. I didn't see anyone else with her.

"Oh hey, there's Becca," I said. "I'm going to say hi."

Dennis didn't reply, nod his head or anything. I was going to repeat myself, but then I remembered that was how he was. It was my biggest pet peeve about him when we were dating and now as friends, that hadn't changed.

I squeezed through the crowd waiting to be seated until I reached Becca.

"Oh my god, Jackie," she said. "How are you?"

Becca hugged me tightly and I hugged her back.

"What was that for?" I asked with a laugh.

"You have no idea how happy I am to see you. I hate waiting in crowded places by myself."

"I don't blame you," I said. "The only thing worse than that is being with a bunch of people and feeling alone."

"Right?" she said with a laugh. "Oh wait, are you here with a group? Because they don't sound like much fun."

"They're alright, I'm probably just being a little sensitive or something. I didn't want to go out tonight."

"New Years Eve is a crazy night to go out," she said. "I can't believe I let him convince me."

"Oh? Him? Is this someone you'll need to give us details on at Mirabella's?" I teased.

"Oh no, absolutely no. It's just Gideon. You guys tease me about him enough."

"Right, Gideon, the sexy, single architect who just so happens to be your very good friend."

She laughed. "Don't start. We are friends."

"Sure, sure. You know if you're friends now you just might be perfect together as a couple," I said.

Becca rolled her eyes and scrunched up her freckled nose.

"What about you and Mr. Best Man billionaire?" she asked.

"Okay, okay, I'll drop the Gideon stuff as long as you don't mention Brent ever again. Deal?"

"Deal," she said.

Becca's eyes moved towards the door and her face lit up. I turned around and saw an attractive, lanky male in his twenties. He ran his fingers through his sandy-colored hair as he looked around. When his eyes found Becca, he winked and grinned devilishly before heading towards us.

If we hadn't just made a deal, I would have busted her chops so bad. There was no way these two were just friends, at least not for long.

"Enjoy your night," I said. "I should get back to my friends before they order without me."

In just the few minutes I spent talking to Becca, Dennis and his friends had been seated. I found their table, but they forgot to tell the hostess their group now had an extra person. As I went to sit in the empty seat, Dennis stood up and waved to me.

"Jackie, over here," he called out.

He grabbed a waitress as she was walking by and motioned to the table and then to me. She called a bus boy, who moved another table over and put down a place setting for me.

As I sat down next to Dennis, he smiled at me then turned and leaned towards his friends. I moved a little closer, trying to hear the conversation, but the restaurant was too loud and I was too far away.

The waiter came and brought everyone drinks, except me. *Had I been talking to Becca that long?* Before he walked away, he came over and stood in front of me as he placed his tray underneath his arm.

"Hi, I'm Trevor," he said. "Would you like to order a drink while you wait?"

He pointed to the empty chair in front of me. I felt so out of sorts that I wasn't sure what he was asking. Did he think I was there alone?

"I'm with them," I said.

Trevor looked over at the group who were laughing at something Dennis said, then shrugged.

"What can I get you?" he asked.

Dennis's friends cheered loudly as they did a round of shots.

"A margarita on the rocks, no salt," I said. "And a glass of water."

I nursed my margarita as the night went on. No one spoke to me, but who could? The restaurant was too loud. Still, I blamed Dennis because he pushed me to go out with them and to sit next to him at the end of the table, away from everyone else.

Trevor the waiter was filling my glass of water when the woman sitting across from Dennis leaned across the table towards me. She had bright blue eyes and short platinum blonde hair that stood out from her caramel skin so much, she reminded me of a candle. Earlier I thought I heard someone called her Penny.

"Dennis said you're a waitress," Penny said. "Bet you're glad you're not working tonight. What restaurant do you work at?"

Dennis turned and answered before I could speak.

"Jackie thinks she's too good to work in a restaurant," he said.

"That's not true," I said. "I just prefer events."

I bit my tongue before I ended up blowing up at him. I hated when he answered for me and I knew what was coming next.

"Doesn't matter," he said. "Either way, it's not a real job. It's what someone does when they can't do anything else."

"Oh? Then maybe you should find somewhere else to stay."

"Boy, you're sensitive tonight," he said. "Maybe you should have stayed home." Dennis turned back towards his friends. "I saved her from sitting around in her shitty apartment."

"My shitty apartment? The one I can't get you out of?"

I waited for him to say something, anything, but it didn't matter. He didn't hear me. He was yucking it up with his friends again.

Not wanting to hear what else Dennis had to say, I sat back in my seat and waited for the dinner to end. I would have gone home if I could, but on New Year's Eve I knew I'd never be able to get a cab.

Maybe I was being sensitive, but if I was it was only because I was done putting up with Dennis.

Sitting by myself at a table for nine wasn't the worst. If anything it was something I had grown used to when we dated. Whenever we were out with someone else Dennis always made me the butt of his jokes and he found ways to put me down. None of it was very obvious and I doubted that anyone ever noticed, but it was something I could count on whenever we were out with other people. Dennis liked being the center of attention.

My meal was good and the waiter was very attentive with me, but not with the rest of the table. It made me feel even more like I was eating alone. There were a few times when I caught the waiter looking in my direction and he'd quickly look away.

He felt bad for me. I could see it in his eyes. It made me feel even worse. If a stranger felt bad for me, why didn't someone I had a relationship with for four years not notice how he was treating me? Maybe he just didn't care.

I didn't have any lingering feelings for Dennis, but I always thought we were friends. Maybe I was wrong. How else could I explain that sitting at a table with eight other people made me feel even more alone? I should've stayed at home.

When the check came, Dennis finally turned towards me. As he leaned towards me, I expected him to ask me for money, but he surprised me.

"Tonight's on me," he said. "Sorry I dragged you out and then hardly talked to you."

"Don't worry about it," I said.

Thinking over my relationship with Dennis, I wondered how I ever thought we were friends. We were barely friends when we dated. Samantha was probably right when she called Dennis a rebound from Marc. When I thought about it I realized I tried to replace Marc with Dennis, even down to our friendship.

"Aren't you forgetting something?" Dennis asked, interrupting my thoughts.

I stared at him blankly. "What?"

"You're so rude you can't even say thank you?"

His tone had acid in it. Usually I would back down and apologize when he made a comment like that, but not anymore.

"Have you ever thanked me for all those times I let you stay with me? Or the many times I brought home lunch or dinner for you?" I stood up, not wanting to be near him anymore. "I'll meet you outside. If I had another way home, I would take it. Oh and that reminds me, you're moving out tomorrow and don't expect to ever stay with me again."

As I headed towards the door, I glanced over at the bar. Standing facing the bar were two men in expensive suits, one with blond hair and the other with dark hair. My stomach churned recognizing Brent and Gunnar.

How is it that everywhere I go he shows up? Damn town is too small!

I thought about how wonderful Brent was when I finally broke down about Marc. But that meant that he, out of everyone, should understand how much being stood up meant to me.

How could he do that? Why didn't he show up for our date?

I pulled my coat around me tightly and continued walking towards the door. I had to stop this. How did I become such a bum magnet? I looked at my watch and saw it was getting closer to midnight.

I was never one of those people who made resolutions, but I promised myself that as of midnight, I would only date great guys. Unless he was worthy of me and my time, he wouldn't get the time of day from me. No more assholes.

As I reached the door, I turned around hoping to get one final glimpse of Brent sitting at the bar, but he wasn't there. Behind me, Dennis's group of friends got stuck behind a waiter.

There were too many people in that section of the restaurant, but I still noticed Brent approaching Dennis. A second later Dennis disappeared as the crowd gasped.

What happened? Did Brent just punch him??

It didn't make sense to me. Why would he hit him? With my heart beating wildly in my chest, I pushed through the crowd to reach them.

Chapter Eighteen

Brent

The bartender poured a couple of glasses of vodka on the rocks and set them down in front of Gunnar and I. The restaurant was packed with the New Year's Eve crowd. Smiling faces drifted past with the constant hum of conversation. It was the last place I wanted to be.

"Aren't you glad I dragged you out?" Gunnar asked.

"Actually no," I said. "I can't believe I gave in to you."

"Don't be such a pussy, man. You said it yourself, you weren't dating, you were just fucking. What do you care if she's got a boyfriend?"

I sighed. "You just don't get it, do you? It was never just fucking to me. Ever. I only did it because I thought maybe if we kept spending time together she'd leave his sorry ass."

"That's the most ridiculous thing I've ever heard. Trust me, if there's one thing I know it's women," Gunnar said.

His gaze shifted to a tall redhead. She smiled at him and he nodded his head once towards her, then once towards the curvy brunette next to her.

"I know what'll get your mind off Jackie," he said.

"No, the last thing I want is to talk to another woman," I said.

"Who said anything about talking?" he said with a grin.

The two women walked over to us. As Gunnar and I rose from our stools to offer them to the ladies, I saw Jackie's boyfriend Dennis walk towards a table with a group of people.

Gunnar introduced the two women to me, but I was so preoccupied with seeing Dennis without Jackie that I didn't hear their names.

Where is she? I wondered. *And why don't I ever see them out together? It's New Year's Eve, why would he go out without her?*

As I turned around and looked towards Dennis's table, Jackie rushed past. She was fresh faced and her hair looked a little messy like it always did after sex.

I clenched my fists as I imagined her with him. I felt like someone stabbed me in the heart as I thought of him touching her soft skin, kissing her sweet lips. Did he even realize what an incredible woman he had?

Gunnar and his friends kept talking, drinks came and went, but my mind was at a table somewhere else in the restaurant. I had no idea how much time had passed, but every few minutes I turned around hoping to get another glimpse of her.

Gunnar placed his hand on my shoulder and leaned towards me.

"What's going on? You haven't said a word since my friends came over," he said.

"She's here," I said.

"She? As in your girl?"

"Exactly, my girl. But she's here with that douchebag."

"Then do something about it. You have your choice of two beautiful women right in front of you but you could care less. For months you've talked about nothing but her, but have you ever told her how you feel?"

He was saying everything I was afraid to say to myself.

"No," I said. "You know that."

"Listen, if it were me, if I was that crazy about a woman, nothing would stop me from making sure everyone knew she was mine."

"Yeah, in a normal situation of course that's what I'd do. But things with Jackie are complicated," I said. "She doesn't even like me."

"Fuck complicated. You're a goddamn idiot if you think any woman would waste a minute of her time with you if she wasn't into you."

I shook my head as I let Gunnar's words penetrate my thick skull. I knew he was right. I knew I was letting every chance I had with Jackie slip away because of whatever she had going on with that guy.

I was so afraid of losing what I had with her that I never told her I loved her. It wasn't about the sex. I wanted her, all of her, all the time.

As I turned around again, I saw the group Dennis came in with leaving. Dennis was hanging back with a woman with bright blonde hair. I looked over the crowd again, trying to find Jackie, but she wasn't there.

Waiting for Jackie to join them, I kept an eye on the group. Dennis slipped his arm around the blonde's waist and whispered into her ear. It was an intimate gesture most people wouldn't notice, but I knew he wouldn't have done it with Jackie there.

The group stopped as a waiter walked past with a large tray of food. Dennis leaned closer to the blonde and kissed her.

"That fucking asshole," I said.

"What's going on?" Gunnar asked as he turned to look.

"He's cheating on her," I said, my fists clenched.

I might not have told Jackie the truth about how I felt, but I'd be damned if I let that guy get away with hurting her.

I pushed my way through the crowd until I was face to face with Dennis.

"Hey, it's Brent, right?" Dennis asked, a big smile plastered on his face.

"This is for Jackie," I said.

My fist collided with his face, sending him onto the floor. The blonde knelt beside him asking if he was okay. Gunnar patted me on the back.

"Oh my god! What's going on?" Jackie said as she pushed through the crowd.

She looked at Dennis still on the floor, rubbing his chin, then turned around to me.

"Brent? You did this?" she asked as confusion spread across her face.

"He kissed her," I said. "No one should be allowed to treat you like that."

"Why would I care who he kisses?" she asked.

"Because you love him," I said between clenched teeth.

It was the hardest thing I ever had to say.

"Love him? Where would you get that idea from?" she asked. "And what would you care anyway? You stood me up."

"Stood you up?" I asked. "What are you talking about?"

Dennis started to get to his feet.

"I think I should get home," he said.

I shoved him back onto the floor as I started to piece things together.

"You're not going anywhere," I said, glaring at him. "Tell her."

"I don't know what you're talking about," Dennis said. "You're just some fucking asshole who punched me for no reason."

"I'm the fucking asshole who punched you because you told me you two were in a relationship. You said you've been together for years and that she said you were the love of her life. Is that true?"

"You said that?" Jackie asked Dennis with her arms wrapped tightly around herself. "When did this happen? When did you talk to Brent?"

"Christmas Eve," I said. "When I came to your apartment to pick you up for dinner."

"You came? I didn't know. Dennis never told me," she said before turning to face Dennis as he rose to his feet again. "Why would you do that?"

"I know guys like him," Dennis said. "I was just protecting you. I--"

I interrupted Dennis before he could say anything more.

"The night of Sam and Drake's wedding, was it you who answered the phone?"

"You called?" she asked.

"I know it's not cool or whatever, but I couldn't wait to talk to you again so I called right away," I said.

Jackie glared at Dennis.

"A man answered the phone and said he was your boyfriend," I said. "He said you like fucking with guy's heads just to see if you can get them to call. He said he didn't care because you always came home to him."

"How could you do this? I was trying to help you out and you lied to me," she snapped at Dennis. "You know how I feel about being stood up. You knew everything it would bring up. I thought we were friends. How could you do something as nice as fill up my car with gas and drop it off for me but then turn around and do something like this?"

"That was me," I said. "You're talking about the day you left your keys in the car, right? I filled your tank and then dropped off the car for you."

"You let me think that was you," she said as her eyes narrowed at Dennis. "You selfish, egotistical asshole! You let me feel sorry for myself. You let me feel like shit."

Jackie's fist flew out and hit Dennis in the stomach. As he buckled over, he looked up towards the blonde who shook her head and walked away.

"No wonder you love her," Gunnar said. "Nothing like a girl with a good right hook."

Gunnar grabbed Dennis by the arm and yanked him towards the door, then pushed him out. His two girlfriends hooked their arms through his and smiled up at him.

"I guess I'll have to keep these two ladies entertained all by myself," Gunnar said as he left.

Jackie stared up at me with her one eyebrow raised.

"You love me?" she asked.

"Gunnar has a big mouth," I said.

"Answer the question."

I put my arm around her, like I had so many other times, and led her outside. The air was crisp, reminding me of snow. No one else was on the street but us. We walked to a bench next to an old-fashioned street lamp and sat down.

"I've never hated you," I said. "From that first moment I met you, I knew there was something special about you. I don't know if it was Sam pushing us together so much or just the way that blue dress hugged your body, but I couldn't get you out of my mind."

"But--"

"Let me finish," I said. "I've been lying to you all this time. I never wanted you just for sex. I just wanted whatever I could have with you. Whatever time I could get with you, that's what I wanted. I didn't understand why you hated me so much. I didn't know why you were screwing around with me when you had Dennis at home, but I didn't care. I just wanted to be with you."

"Dennis and I haven't been together in over a year," she said. "I was just helping him out."

"You don't need to explain anything to me," I said. "I just wish I was honest with you sooner. We've been spending all this time together and all I had to do was ask you about Dennis or tell you that I called that night and things would have been different. Instead I let you continue thinking that I didn't like you when that couldn't be further from the truth."

"And what Gunnar said?" she asked.

"It's true. I love you. I've had feelings for you for a while, but I think that day when you saw Marc and opened up was it for me."

"That was such a bad day," she said, her face softening. "But there you were, the man I hated for no reason at all, and...I don't know, but that was the day that I realized I couldn't be without you."

"That's why I asked you to Ashley and Xander's Christmas party. I was done with our charade. I was going to tell you everything that night, but when I arrived at your house, Dennis told me you didn't want to see me anymore. I was an idiot to believe him, but he confirmed what I believed already."

Jackie looked at her watch.

"It's almost midnight," she said. "Do you ever make any resolutions?"

I pulled out my phone and found a site with Times Square live. As I slipped my arm around her shoulders, I slid closer to her.

"I do," I said. "Every year I promise myself I'm going to do more to help those who can't help themselves. It's not your traditional resolution, but it keeps me grounded."

"That makes me feel like my resolution is stupid," she said with a small laugh.

"Whatever your resolution is, I'm sure it's not stupid. As long as it means something to you, it's important."

She nodded slowly and I could see that she was thinking.

I turned the volume of my phone up as the countdown began. As the ball reached the bottom, the restaurant erupted with noisemakers and cheers. I leaned closer and kissed Jackie's forehead.

"Happy New Year," I said.

"Happy New Year, Brent."

She smiled at me and I knew I would do anything to make her happy for the rest of her life.

"I have a new proposition for you," I said.

Epilogue

Six Months Later

Jackie

It was a perfect June day in Canyon Cove. The sun was beginning to set into the Pacific Ocean and one of my best friends was sitting on a lounge chair beside me, holding my hand. Things couldn't be better.

We were in matching chairs, on the sand, the orange haze of the sun glittered perfectly off the calm blue water. Dressed in shorts, we decided to take a break after a long walk on the beach. A year ago I felt empty, but that was a long time ago.

Shade hopped onto the long portion of my chair and curled himself into a tight ball.

"He really has no idea how large he is," I said as I tried to figure out where to put my legs.

"What are you talking about? Look at how small he is," Brent said. "Right, Shade?"

Shade wagged his thick tail excitedly, causing a faint thud every time his tail hit my thigh.

"I'm pretty sure this is abuse," I said, laughing.

"Take it up with him. I didn't do a thing."

In the distance a couple stood facing each other, the breeze gently tousling their hair. They held each other's hands as they exchanged wedding vows on the pier. Brent pointed over to them.

"What do you think?" he asked.

"What do you mean?"

"A happy couple getting married. I think that should be us."

My phone buzzed in my bag before I could say anything.

"You should check that," Brent said. "I've been hearing it buzzing all afternoon. It could be something important."

"It's nothing important," I said. "It's probably someone trying to get me to fill in for them at the last minute."

I pulled my phone out of my bag and saw several texts messages from hours ago.

Becca: Where are you?

Ashley: Are you running late? We're waiting for you. Sam is looking hangry though lol!

I read Ashley's text to Brent and he laughed.

"Hangry? Hungry *and* angry? You don't want to be near Sam when she's like that," he said, laughing.

Samantha: We're at Mirabella's, where are you? I thought you were coming.

I felt bad about forgetting about our Mirabella's lunch, but I knew there would be others. It had been a long time since I missed one of the Mirabella lunches. They were fine without me.

After I graduated in May, Brent finally convinced me to move in with him. It was a strange thing for me after being on my own for so long, but since we made it official, I rarely slept at my apartment anyway.

I was busy apologizing to my friends for missing the lunch when Brent leaned closer and peeked at my phone.

"Did you get any other texts?" Brent asked.

"Mmm hmm. I just haven't gotten to it yet."

"Who's it from?" he asked.

"I don't know," I said, looking at the unfamiliar number in my message list. "Let me check."

I tapped the message and it opened to a photo of Shade. He was wearing the same bandana around his neck that Brent put on him that morning.

"That's odd," I said. "Why would someone send me a picture of Shade?"

"Maybe they're trying to tell you something," he said. "Look closer at the picture."

"Did you do this? This is just weird," I murmured as I looked at the photo.

Shade smiled in the picture with his tongue dangling out of his mouth. His warm brown eyes looked happy like always. I had no idea what I was supposed to be looking at.

"Did you take this?" I asked. "This isn't your number."

Brent sighed impatiently.

"Wait a minute," I mumbled before enlarging the picture. "Is there something on his bandana?"

Brent's face was blank, but as I looked at him the edges of his mouth tugged into a grin.

"It's been there all day," he said. "I thought for sure you were going to see it when you were petting him earlier."

"There's something on his bandana? You put something on there?"

I tried to make out what it was in the picture, but it was too blurry. All I could see was something blue that reflected the light.

"Come here, Shade," I said, holding my arms out to him. "Turn around, buddy."

He wagged his tail again but didn't budge.

"Let's go, come on, come just a little closer," I said, reaching for his bandana.

Shade wiggled as his tail beat faster against my leg. He touched his nose against my hand and I reached out for the bandana and lifted it off his head.

I spun the bandana around, looking for whatever was attached to it. Out of the corner of my eye, Brent waited impatiently.

Nearby, a large seagull dove towards a table the couple had set up with food. It cackled loudly until it got a response in the distance. As the bird waddled along the pier, he was joined by a smaller one.

"Why are you looking at me like that?" I asked, tilting my head to the side.

"You're killing me, you know that?" Brent grabbed the bandana and held up a deep blue sapphire ring with channel set diamonds.

I knew what it was as soon as I recognized something was glittering in the picture, but sometimes I just enjoyed driving Brent crazy.

I smiled as I took the ring from him, then reached down to pet Shade.

"It's beautiful, Shade. I love it."

Brent shook his head as he laughed.

"Jackie, even with the ups and downs of this past year, I wouldn't change anything. Well, maybe I'd change the whole Dennis thing," he teased.

"That was definitely the down part. You're going to hold that against me, aren't you?"

"Maybe," he said, smirking. "But only if it means you owe me."

"Oh boy, here we go again," I said. "What's your proposition this time?"

"This time, I'm proposing. But before you say anything, let me say something."

I nodded hesitantly. Brent and I had talked about marriage before. Brent was excited to get married, but I was worried things would change between us. I loved him and I wanted to marry him one day, but things had been so great between us I didn't want to mess that up.

"We've been together for six months," he said. "And instead of calling that an engagement ring, I want to call that a promise ring. I promise to love you, appreciate you, and do whatever I can to always make you happy. You know I can be impulsive, but I've been really thinking about this a lot."

"So you're just going to wait until I say I'm ready?"

"I know you're mine. Nothing is going to change that," he said.

He leaned closer and touched his forehead to mine before gently kissing my lips.

I put the ring on and looked into Brent's grey eyes.

I thought back to the day of Samantha and Drake's wedding when Brent said life was too short to be serious. He was right, life was too short.

There was nothing I was more confident about in my life than being with Brent. Everything was so easy with him. He made me laugh, he dried my tears, he made me realize that I was worthy of a good relationship. And that was what I had with him.

"I remember when I thought you hated me," I said.

"I never hated you," he said. "Admit it, you still hate me."

My mouth curved into a smile.

"I do," I said. "I think I hate you more every day."

Nearby, the newly married couple clinked glasses of champagne with their guests. They looked so happy that it reminded me of Samantha and Drake.

Samantha's words flitted through my mind--

It's made me realize how Drake and I could've been together even longer. I wasted time away from him when I could have been happy instead. I want that happiness for you.

I wanted that happiness too. And I wanted it for a lifetime. I knew I had that with Brent and nothing would ever change that.

"What are you thinking about?" Brent asked.

I pointed at the small wedding and the minister quietly leaving.

"What do you think?" I asked.

"Are you serious?"

"Ask me," I said.

"Will you marry me?"

"Yes," I said.

"Now?"

"Yes!"

Brent wrapped his arms around me and hugged me tight. Then he stood and took my hand as we raced over to the minister.

We caught up to him and asked if he could marry us right there and then. He scrunched his face as he looked at us, and I was sure he was going to say no, but then he nodded with understanding.

"I don't know how legal this is, but why not?" he said. "I can see the love you have for one another."

With the sun making orange streaks in the sky as it sank into the Pacific, Brent and I exchanged our vows. It was just the two of us in shorts, with Shade as our witness and it was perfect.

About The Author

Liliana Rhodes is a New York Times and USA Today Bestselling Author who writes Contemporary and Paranormal Romance. Blessed with an overactive imagination, she is always writing and plotting her next stories. She enjoys movies, reading, photography, listening to music, and spending time with her son. After growing up in the Northeast, Liliana now lives in the Southeast with her husband, son, two very spoiled dogs, and a parrot and a fish who are plotting to take over the world.

Connect Online

www.LilianaRhodes.com

www.facebook.com/AuthorLilianaRhodes

Made in the USA
Middletown, DE
21 June 2018